THE TAINTED LENS

Karin Harrison

ISBN: 1533677719
ISBN-13: 9781533677716
Hofgarten Press
Printed in the United States of America

Book cover: Beacon of Hope by Alexandra Kopp

To my children,
Susan, Tim and Philip,
with all my love.

ACKNOWLEDGEMENTS

Thanks to my editors, Ted M. Zurinsky and Adele Brinkley,
for their thorough editing, and catching the many
errors I made.

CHAPTER 1

———

KYLE LEANED BACK IN HIS chair, yawned, and pushed the laptop back. The kitchen clock indicated twelve midnight. A swath of light brown hair fell onto his forehead, and he pushed it aside, and rubbed his eyes. He'd been writing all day, but now his report was completed and ready to be delivered to the paper. The energy that had carried him through the day was rapidly fading. He rose, opened the small pantry and his eyes fell on a can of chicken soup probably left there by a previous tenant. It took less than five minutes to heat it. He gulped it down and strolled over to the sofa, dropped onto it, and fell asleep immediately.

He woke midmorning. Thinking he'd heard a scream, he raised his head and listened. Must have been a seagull. After he drank a cup of instant coffee, he reached for his camera. Today was his last day at Marshall Point Light. His job was done, but he wanted to climb the platform one last time, take one last photo. He stepped outside the apartment. A chilly wind enveloped him and struck his face. The heavy cloud cover filling the sky threatened an early snow. He pulled up his collar and skipped down the steps. Turning toward the bridge leading to the beacon, he noticed the door to the gift shop was wide open. He glanced at the parking lot where Melanie's car sat undisturbed. He decided to check on Melanie, and entered the gift shop. When he didn't see her, he called out, "Hey, Melanie, where are you?" He walked around the counter and spotted a woman's shoe on the floor, and the last thing he saw was Melanie, stretched out on her side, her head resting in a puddle of blood.

A rumbling noise woke Kyle as be bounced up and down in the dark. He turned his head and winced; pain spasms shot through his head. He struggled to sit up when he felt the constraints tied around his wrists and ankles. A cotton hood covered his head. He inhaled deeply.

"Who are you? What do you want with me?" No answer. "Where are we going?" he said. The hood muffled his words.

"Shut the hell up, if you know what's good for you," the voice barked.

The jeep travelled at high speed. Kyle lay back and tried to piece together what had happened when the memory of Melanie's bloodied head rose before his eyes. *I'm being kidnapped.* The thought hit him with ferocity, and fear threatened to paralyze his body. What was going to happen to him? He was certain Melanie was dead. Would he be next? At this moment the right tires hit a hole in the road, jolting Kyle to the driver's side, and he passed out.

The jeep came to screeching halt. Kyle moaned. His head ached and his cramped body protested in agony. He needed to stretch. The door slammed as Kyle held his breath and waited. When the hood was pulled off his head, Kyle squinted. In front of him stood a man, maybe 6'1 and wearing blue jeans and a sweatshirt, his face covered with a mask revealing only his eyes, nose, and mouth.

"Where am I?" Kyle demanded. "Untie my hands."

The man didn't answer and proceeded to untie Kyle's legs instead.

"What do want with me?" Kyle demanded.

"Shut up," the man said and yanked Kyle out of the jeep. Kyle swayed to catch his balance. He stood facing a rundown cabin with a lean-to woodshed. He looked around. They were in the middle of a forest. The snow fell heavily, adding more coverage to the white mantled trees and cottage.

The man pushed Kyle toward the lean-to and yanked the door open. "Get in," he growled. Kyle lowered his head and staggered inside. A push from behind sent him flying onto a wooden cot. The door slammed shut, and Kyle heard the mechanics of a padlock being put in place.

He moaned as he rolled over and struggled to sit up. Narrow streams of light forced their way between the wall boards of the shed. Except for a potbelly stove and the wooden cot, the place was empty. He got to his feet and approached the door. He pushed his body against it, but to no avail. The construction appeared flimsy enough, however it held strong. With one eye, he peered through a crack between the door and the frame. A dense forest of pine trees stretched as far as he could see. He guessed the path leading to the cabin must be located somewhere to the left, out of his view.

He turned and stumbled over to the cot and sat on the dirty, rough blanket. His mind raced. *What does this creep want with me?* The crime scene replayed over and over in his head. Closing his eyes, he tried to push the image of Melanie's body out of his mind. Fear chilled him. *Will I be killed as well?* As he leaned back and pulled the blanket around him as best he could, he heard the crunching of footsteps in the snow. The door opened and the man entered carrying a stack of firewood and dropped it onto the floor. He wore the same mask.

"I'll get the fire started. You'll have to keep it fed. If you're running out of wood, holler." His eyes appraised Kyle up and down. "You a photographer or somethin'?"

"What's it to you?" Kyle replied with a huff as he got to his feet. The slug on the chin flung him against the wall with such force, he bounced back. He groaned. Blood seeped into his mouth from a cut on his lip and trickled down his chin.

"I ask the questions here," the man snapped. "Now, one more time. What do you do and where do you do it?"

"I'm a photojournalist. I work for the *Portland Journal*."

"Uh. That looks like an expensive camera. I'll be sure to get at least $500 at the pawnshop."

"You're going to pawn my camera?"

"Yes, and I expect to get a lot more money, thanks to you." After he had finished loading the stove with kindling and lit the fire, he slammed the iron door shut. "You best keep the stove fed; otherwise you'll freeze to death out here." The man snickered and turned to leave.

Kyle rose. "Wait. Can you at least untie me? I'll be locked in. I can't go anywhere," he pleaded.

The man stood still. Then he turned, approached Kyle, and pushed him roughly onto the cot. He pulled out a switch blade and cut the ropes binding Kyle's wrists. "If you wanna stay alive, you'd better give me no trouble," he muttered and left the shed. The door banged and Kyle heard the lock click again.

Kyle needed to pee, and he searched the dismal interior. He spotted a bucket in the corner. Afterward he crept back onto the cot. Exhaustion claimed him, but restful sleep was not granted and he drifted in and out of memories of times long past.

The alarm on his cell phone jarred Kyle out of his sleep. His eyes still closed, he reached over to the gray acacia night stand and shut it off. He jumped out of bed and crossed the floor to the open window. The air felt brisk and clean, and he took a deep breath. The beach was deserted except for one man strolling at the water's edge in his bare feet. Kyle grinned and reached for his camera. His dad took a walk every morning without fail. "It helps me get my head together," he said.

Kyle focused his camera and pulled back in horror. His dad had collapsed. He dropped the camera onto the bed, grabbed his jeans and raced out the door.

"Mom!" He stepped into his pants as he navigated down the stairs. "Mom!" he screamed. His mother came running from the kitchen, while his younger brother, Luke, appeared sleepy-eyed at the upstairs landing.

"Call an ambulance. It's Dad!" He flew through the kitchen door and ran down the beach. His dad lay on his side, the water lapping at his feet. Kyle dragged him away from the water's edge. He dropped to his knees and placed his ear against his dad's mouth. Sensing a faint breath, he immediately began CPR.

The ambulance took him away ten minutes later, followed by Kyle, driving his dad's car. His mom and Luke sat quietly, their eyes filled with fear. They arrived at Graceville Memorial Hospital shortly and watched the medics hurry his dad down the hall and disappear behind two large blue doors.

The morning news blared from the TV as Joan sat dry-eyed between her sons, their hands firmly clasped. Luke was crying softly.

"He'll be fine, Mom. He survived Desert Storm. He'll get through this," Kyle said.

She nodded mutely and squeezed his hand. She desperately wanted to believe Gregg would live. She turned to her sons. "Let's pray for him."

They bowed their heads, but Kyle wasn't into religion. If there was a God, why did he allow such misery? How much did his father matter to a God who had so many people calling upon him, more important people. He glanced at his mother. Her lips moved in silent prayer, and for a moment he wished he could believe like she did.

The door opened and the cardiologist, his face grim, entered. Kyle rose immediately while his mom remained seated, beads of sweat lining her forehead. The doctor stood in front of them. "I'm so sorry. We did everything we could. Gregg had a massive heart attack. He was gone by the time the ambulance arrived at the hospital. We were unable to revive him."

Joan's body folded, and she slipped from the chair. Kyle grabbed her in time and held her closely to him. They wept quietly. The doctor stood and watched them with his head bowed. He felt their pain. It was never easy to lose a patient.

Joan pulled away from Kyle. She wiped her face with her hand and said, "Can we see him?"

"Of course. Follow me."

———————

The sun lit up the beach, with the promise of a bright spring day. Kyle listened to the incoming tide pounding the shore in a steady rhythm to the cries of the seagulls wheeling above the surf. It had been three months since they had buried his dad. Life had never been the same for the Weldon family, and each member was coping differently. Luke had accepted the inevitable and was moving on. His mom vacillated between the present and the past. She talked about Gregg every day. Kyle found himself taking over some of his dad's responsibilities and trying to be supportive to his mother and brother. He harbored deep resentment at his father's premature death.

"Who is God?" he said to Joan one evening after supper. "Someone who has the power to play with our lives, to create pain and suffering while he sits back and gloats?"

"Oh no, Kyle, no. God is good. You have to believe things happen for a reason."

"I see no sense in what happened to us. Look at you, Mom. You are miserable. You and Dad should have been allowed to grow old together. Luke needs a father, *I* need him." He covered his face and his head dropped to the table. His shoulders trembled, and for the first time since the funeral his tears flowed freely.

Kyle sighed. Another sleepless night spent tossing and turning, and facing a busy day did little for his disposition. Might as well get out of bed. In the shower, he relished the hot water massaging his lanky frame. His smile turned into a frown as he recalled last night's humiliation. *Maybe I'm unemployed right now and don't know it.*

He was thrilled when Mr. Rappel, the owner of The Old Mill Inn, hired him as a busboy a month ago. Wilma, the chef, a short, stocky woman with a big heart, took him under her wing from the start. He talked to her about the loss of his father and the gap that had been created in his life. He saw his mother bravely carry on, but he sensed her pain. Wilma helped put things into perspective by relating her experience when her husband, a fireman, was killed while on duty, and she found herself alone, raising a teenager. In turn Kyle learned how to give his mom the support she needed.

A senior in high school, Kyle worked five nights a week while struggling to keep up with his homework. He had no time for a social life, but he never complained because he knew the challenges his mom faced taking care of him and Luke.

Kyle's vintage Chevy devoured most of his income. Currently, it sat in the driveway until he could afford a new muffler. He had a long way to go before he could save up the $350 repair cost quoted by Joe, his mechanic.

He turned off the shower and reached for the towel. Below, the door slammed. Luke left to catch the school bus. Kyle watched from his window as Luke kicked at the walnuts on the ground. They sailed like golf balls across the lawn. Kyle grinned, and he reached for his pants. A car pulled into the driveway. Lisa had arrived.

"Kyle, time to leave," his mom called from downstairs. He finished dressing and bounced down the steps. He wolfed down a Pop Tart and grabbed his books.

"Bye, Mom." Brushing her cheek with a kiss, he hurried out the door.

"Morning, Kyle." Lisa greeted him with fluttering eyelids, and he gave her a crooked smile. He knew she had a crush on him, but he had no interest in a relationship. He couldn't spare the time. He had made his plans a long time ago. Soon, he would graduate from high school and go on to college to pursue a degree in photojournalism. The camera was his passion. He had to make sure Lisa didn't misinterpret his acceptance to be chauffeured by her while his car was out of commission.

"Hey, Lisa." Slipping into the passenger seat, he looked at the gas gauge and said, "You need gas."

"I know. I'll stop at Joe's." She slowed down at the end of the long driveway to wave to Luke who was waiting for the school bus. "How's it going, Luke?"

"Hey, Lisa…"

"There's your bus." Lisa pointed to the highway where the bus was approaching and slowly came to a halt. "See you, Luke." Lisa pulled out onto the road. When they reached the gas station, Kyle jumped out of the car.

"Ten bucks, no more," Lisa said as she pulled out her wallet.

"I'll take care of it."

When he finished pumping the gas, Kyle went inside to the mechanic's desk to pay the bill. He frowned as he pulled the ten dollar bill from his wallet. He had $20 left to last him the rest of the week. He desperately needed to get his hands on some money.

"Morning, Kyle." Joe said with a wide grin. "I see you and Lisa are getting mighty friendly."

Handing him the money, Kyle said, "Not really. She's giving me a ride until my car's fixed." Before Joe could say another word, Kyle fled, leaving Joe chuckling.

They arrived at school, and Lisa parked the car. "I can give you a ride to and from work tonight. It'll give your mom a break," she said.

Turning his head, he looked at her soft, round face. For the first time, he took notice of her large brown eyes beneath perfect brows and the way her mouth curved with tenderness when she spoke to him. "Are you allowed to be out that late?"

"Yes. My parents told me they're pleased I've offered to help. There's no problem."

He didn't answer.

"I don't mind," she said quietly. "Wouldn't you do the same for me?"

"Yeah, I guess so." He climbed out of the car. "See you tonight." He strolled across the lawn to join two buddies standing beneath the huge elm tree in front of the school building and smoking cigarettes.

"Hey, Kyle, what's up?" Bobby, a tall fellow with spiked hair greeted him, while the other boy, Tony, whipped out a pack of cigarettes, pointing it at Kyle.

"Why not? Thanks." Kyle took a cigarette and pulled a lighter from his pocket. He lit up, inhaled deeply, and then shuddered. He never really liked smoking.

The school bell rang, and they flicked their cigarettes and hurried inside the building.

————◆————

After Lisa dropped him off at the restaurant that evening, Mr. Rappel met him inside. "I need to talk to you," he said.

Kyle's heart sank when Mr. Rappel gestured for him to follow. Since Mr. Rappel had not witnessed the incident, Kyle had hoped he might escape his employer's wrath, but the grim expression on Mr. Rappel's face indicated otherwise.

"Close the door," he snapped after they entered the tidy, compact office. Mr. Rappel walked over to his desk, turned, and said, "I'm appalled at your behavior yesterday, Kyle. You should know better."

"I'm very sorry. The whole thing was an accident."

"I understand that, but you used poor judgment when you tried to wipe the clam chowder from the lady's sweater. What on earth were you thinking?" Mr. Rappel shook his head in frustration. Kyle bit his tongue to control a sudden attack of laughter. He meant well when he used a napkin to blot the soup dripping down her chest after he spilled it onto her sweater. The resounding slap to his face had made him jerk and flush red. The memory of the brief contact with her large, firm breasts lay vivid in his mind.

"I swear, Mr. Rappel, it'll never happen again."

Mr. Rappel remained silent for a moment. "All right," he said, "Up until now, you've been doing a pretty good job, but if anything like this happens again, you're out of here. Now, get to work."

The evening passed quickly, and the restaurant closed after the last stragglers departed the bar area. The busy night left Kyle pleased with his tips. Waiting for his ride, he was helping Wilma clean up when his cell phone rang.

"Kyle."

He strained to listen. Lisa was clearly distressed. "My car won't start. Dad says I need a new battery. I'm so sorry I can't give you a ride home."

"Don't worry. I'll walk. It's only three miles. I've done it before." He disconnected.

Leaving the restaurant, he checked his watch: Midnight. He looked up at the clear, moonlit sky. He smiled when he located the Big Dipper surrounded by millions of glittering stars. The night sky always inspired his imagination as he pondered the mysteries of an infinite universe. Chilled by the brisk air, he pulled up his collar and started to walk. He reached the main road leaving Graceville and noticed the hush lingering across the deserted highway. The little seashore town slept undisturbed. Thirty minutes later, right before he got to the turn leading to his house, he spotted a vehicle on the side of the road. A man waved a dim flashlight inside the trunk.

"Evening," Kyle said.

Twisting his head, the man pointed the dying beam at Kyle's face. He was in his early fifties, Kyle guessed, burly, white-whiskered, and sporting a crew cut. Dressed in a suit and tie, his hand was firmly wrapped around the tire iron.

"What's wrong?" Kyle said, moving closer.

"Got a flat. On top of that, my cell phone died." He muttered a curse.

"You want some help?"

"Yes, as a matter of fact, I do. I'm on my way to Portland. It's my daughter's birthday." He glanced at his watch. "Was my daughter's birthday," he mumbled and stepped aside. Kyle grabbed the spare and the jack and went to the driver's side. The man breathed a sigh of relief as he watched Kyle crouching on the ground. Kyle worked without speaking. He disengaged the greasy lug nuts and replaced the flat with the spare.

"What are you doing out on the road this late, son?" the man asked.

"Just finished work."

"Don't you go to school?"

"Yeah." Kyle fastened the hubcap and slapped the dirt off his hands. "I'll graduate this year." He rose and stretched his back. "You're good to go." Securing the damaged tire and the jack inside the trunk, he turned to the man. "There's a 24-hour gas station about three miles down the road. Joe's Gas and Service. You can't miss it. They'll fix the tire for you."

"Thanks, I'll be fine now." The man reached for his wallet, but Kyle had already walked away.

"What's your name?" the man called after him.

"Kyle Weldon."

"Can I at least give you a lift?"

Kyle turned and walked backwards. "No thanks. It's only a short way." He waved and crossed the road.

———◆———

"Kyle," his mom's voice reached him from afar. Opening his eyes, he stared into her face. "There's a call for you. It's Joe from the gas station."

"What does he want? It's Saturday, the only day I get to sleep late." He turned on his stomach and pounded the pillows.

"He said it's important."

"All right." He swung his long legs onto the floor and walked downstairs.

"Yeah Joe…"

"Hey, buddy, beautiful mornin', ain't it?" Joe's cheerful tone made Kyle cringe.

"I'm tired. What's up?"

"A guy stopped by here last night for a tire repair. He asked about you, and we got to talking about your Chevy. You know the one with the muffler problem?"

"Get to the point, Joe."

"Well, this gentleman thought so highly of you, he wrote a check to cover the muffler repair."

Kyle's ears perked. "Come again? He paid for all of it?"

"Yep. Bring old Betsy in, and we'll fix her up. Cheers." Joe hung up.

Kyle turned to his mother who was fixing breakfast. He opened his mouth to speak, but she said, "I know. Joe told me." She walked over to him and hugged him tightly. "I'm so pleased, Kyle. It was a kind thing you did. The gentleman told Joe meeting you renewed his faith in the young people of today." Tears welling in her eyes, she added, "Your father would be so proud of you."

"I could tell he didn't have a clue how to change a tire."

Joan stepped back and smiled. At times like these, he reminded her so much of his father, a generous, kind man, who loved life and his family. She sighed and popped two slices of bread into the toaster.

"By the way," she said, "The prom is coming up. Who's going to be your date?"

He didn't answer.

"Lisa is hoping…"

"I'm not taking a date."

She spun around. "Why not?"

"Look, Mom, I like Lisa, but I don't want to encourage her. She'll find someone to take her." Avoiding her eyes, he ran his fingers through his hair. He remained quiet for a long time and then said, "I might as well tell you now. I have no intention of spending the rest of my life in Graceville. After I graduate from college, I'm leaving for New York. You know I want to be a photojournalist. Taking pictures is all I've ever wanted to do, and I'm good at it." He strode out of the kitchen.

Stunned, she stared after him. "What's that got to do with going to the prom?" Loudly, she added seconds later, "And what's wrong with Graceville?"

CHAPTER 2

KYLE SLAMMED THE BOOK SHUT. Tomorrow he would take his last final, and he could cram no more into his brain tonight. Snoring, his roommate, Tony, stretched out on the bed, fully dressed, had been asleep for hours. They had been friends since high school. Smith University, PA, had been Tony's third choice, and his parents were relieved after he had been accepted. Not as studious as Kyle, Tony, nevertheless, got passing grades thanks to Kyle's good influence.

Kyle undressed and went to bed. He closed his eyes, but sleep did not come. He would soon begin a new phase in his life. The last four years had streaked by. He had worked hard toward his degree. Once he got through tomorrow, did well on this exam...his lids closed, and he slept.

On graduation day, the sky opened up to a magnificent blue. The warm spring sunshine enveloped the graduates and their families crowding the campus of the small university.

Joined by Tony and his parents, Kyle, Joan, and Luke had gathered on the grounds after the ceremony.

"This is a huge milestone in your lives," Tony's dad said. He turned to Kyle. "I'm grateful to you for keeping an eye on my boy."

"Dad," Tony said and rolled his eyes.

"Why don't we get a bite to eat," Joan said.

"Good idea," Luke said. "I'm starved." He had been checking out the girls wearing their gowns and caps and began flirting with a pretty brunette standing nearby.

Watching him, Kyle said, "I think you're a little out of your league, little brother. These girls are used to dating men."

"Wanna bet?" Luke said and grinned.

The group walked toward the parking lot.

"Lisa wanted to come today, but she had already started her job at Mother Goose Day Care," Joan said.

Kyle didn't reply, just shrugged his shoulders.

"She told me she loves working with children." Joan glanced at her son. "She's really fond of you, Kyle."

Kyle scowled and said. "That's good."

Joan raised her eyebrows, and he quickly added, "Look, Mom, can we drop it?"

Lisa kept in touch with Joan, and she had revealed she and Kyle had been emailing each other. While Lisa always responded quickly, it took weeks before Kyle got back to Lisa. Joan realized he didn't want a serious relationship, and he never mentioned any girls he met at college. Joan smiled to herself. *He's young. Plenty of time to get involved. It's a good thing he's concentrating on his studies.*

After dinner they drove back to Kyle's dorm where he loaded up his mom's car.

"That's it," he said and closed the packed trunk. The back seat was crammed as well. *It's amazing how much stuff I've collected in four years.* He had enough boxes left to fill up his own car along with his precious camera equipment, which he kept within reach at all times. He guessed the collection of pictures he had taken during his time at college numbered in the thousands. He had joined the school newspaper when he was a freshman, and his photos and stories appeared frequently in the monthly publication. Some of his work had been published in national magazines.

He walked around the car and hugged Joan. "Thanks, Mom, for hauling this stuff home. I'll see you in a day or two."

"I wish you'd come home with us today," she said. Kyle remained quiet and she continued, "I know there's still some partying to be done." She gave him a wink and added, "Please be careful."

"Don't worry." He kissed her on the cheek and then turned to Luke and squeezed his arm. "See you, my man."

"Bye." Joan drove off.

Kyle hurried up the steps and entered his room. Tony sat on his bed and pointed to his watch. "We're going to be late for the party."

"Got the booze?"

"Everything's right here." He pulled a brown bag out of the closet. "Beer and Jack Daniels and most importantly, this." He picked up a clear envelope filled with pot, and stuck it in Kyle's face.

"You know I don't fool with this stuff," Kyle said. "Gimme my beer and I'm happy."

"You don't know what you're missing, pal." Tony held the bag to his nose and sniffed.

Kyle smiled. "Let's go, pothead."

They arrived at the large Victorian style house converted into a dorm for girls. The stained glass window above the front door highlighted the pale blue paint of the exterior. Inside was a kitchen, a large living room with an ornate fireplace the girls seldom used, a bathroom on the first, and another on the second floor. The furnishings represented a mix of styles and showed plenty of wear. Eight girls shared the four bedrooms. They kept the house clean, and each one added her personal touch throughout the house. They were told the house was haunted and at one point engaged a paranormal team who detected no ghosts, much to the disappointment of the girls.

Carrying a bottle of beer, Jillian ran out the door to meet Kyle. "You're late." She pulled him close and whispered, "My room-mate has already left for home." She nibbled on Kyle's ear, then turned and pulled him along as she headed for the stairs.

"Hey, wait a minute. The party hasn't even started yet."

"Who cares?" She hiccupped. "Tomorrow we're going to leave this joint forever. Who knows if we ever see each other again? Let's make the most of it while we can." They had reached the landing when Kyle turned, his hands cupped her face, and he kissed her. She pulled away. "Come on," she urged and opened a door. She dragged him inside and kicked the door shut. She grabbed his shirt, and buttons went flying. He unzipped her jeans, and they fell onto the bed. He pulled her T-shirt over her head. She wore no bra, and he cupped her full breasts. She moaned and pushed her body into his. Sex was Jillian's favorite past time, and she never got enough of it.

Afterward, she curled into the curve of his body. "Oh, Kyle," she sighed, "I'm going to miss this."

———◆———

CHAPTER 3

"Morning, Mom." Kyle yawned as he stepped into the sunlit kitchen.

"Morning." Joan sat at the table rummaging through a manila folder.

"What you got there?"

"Scholarship applications for Luke." Their financial situation was dire. She had to go deep into debt to pay Kyle's tuition. Vince Rappel offered her a job managing the books at The Old Mill Inn, and she had accepted gratefully.

"Mr. Rappel put me in contact with a local organization that helps students who are having trouble meeting their tuition."

"Mr. Rappel is taking quite an interest in you since you started to work for him. What's he after?"

Putting down the paper she had been reading and looking up, Joan said, "Does he have to be after something? He's trying to help. We're friends. We've known each other since high school. He's having a hard time since his wife's death last year." Her eyes got dreamy as she continued. "We used to double date, your father and I, and Vincent and Vera."

"V and V," Kyle mused.

Joan smiled. "Yes, that's what we used to call them, V and V. She was a beautiful woman. Everywhere we went, she attracted attention. She was crazy about Vince, and he about her."

"Why didn't they have children?"

"They tried. I remember when Vince took over the restaurant after his father retired, they briefly discussed adoption, but nothing ever came of it."

"Hmm." In his mind Kyle tried to picture Mr. Rappel rocking a baby. He had always treated him well when he worked at his restaurant, but Kyle labeled him grumpy and cantankerous, except when it came to the customers. Mr. Rappel's impeccable manner impressed all of his patrons.

"Did you call the editor at The *Graceville Register* today?"

Kyle flinched. Pouring milk over his cereal, he remained silent. Joan put down her pen and stared at his back. "Kyle, what's wrong?" she asked.

He turned, carrying the bowl over to the table and sitting down next to her. "Yes, Mom, I did. I'll see him today. I'm hoping he'll hire me as a stringer. I don't want to work full time at the *Register.* I'll be nothing but a copyboy, lunch-fetcher, and overall peon. I have a degree in photojournalism. I want to take pictures. It's what I'm good at and what I love to do." He avoided her eyes as he spoke. "I want to go to New York, try to find a job there. I want to photograph people, events, and places. Nothing of importance ever happens in Graceville. I want to be able to sell my work to journals and news media organizations." His cheeks flushed, and his eyes met hers. "Imagine having my pictures published in *National Geographic* or presented on TV." He threw up his arms. "There's no way I'm going to be stuck in small town Graceville working at the *Register* where no one ever leaves unless they retire or drop dead."

Speechless, she looked at him. He had mentioned moving before, but she hoped he would change his mind. *I don't want him to leave.* Tears filled her eyes and she lowered her head. "I guess I'm being unfair. I know you have to live your own life, and it isn't wrong to be ambitious. Your father would have encouraged you to follow your dream, and so must I."

Yet she couldn't resist giving it one last shot. "Working for The *Graceville Register* would give you an opportunity to gather some experience before you move on to Portland or even New York."

"New York is where I need to go."

"You'll need money."

Money. The thought niggled at him as he toyed with his spoon. *She's right. I need money to live on until I land a job. I could always find work at a restaurant, better yet a bar. Yes, I need to work at a bar.* Tony's face popped into his mind. Tony, his college buddy, worked as a bartender at the Iron Fist Tavern here in Graceville while searching for a teaching job at local high schools.

That evening he pulled up in front of the Iron Fist Tavern, parked his car, and went inside. A chatter of voices resonated through the dimly lit, low-ceilinged room. He dropped onto one of the few empty chairs at the bar. At the other end, Tony was conversing with a patron when he spotted Kyle and hurried to greet him.

"Hey, buddy, what're you doing here? Drowning your sorrow over Jillian?" he said and grinned.

"Jillian who?" Kyle replied.

"I guess the love affair is over."

"Love never entered into the picture, and you know it."

"Well, it's good to see you, buddy. What'll it be? The first drink's on the house."

"Give me a beer."

"Coming right up."

Kyle looked around and studied the colorful group of people hanging around the bar. He spotted an elderly gentleman dressed in a suit and tie, sitting with a beautiful woman young enough to be his daughter and engaging in whispered conversation. Two women wearing provocative clothing and too much make-up occupied the table next to them. They scrutinized the men lined up at the bar.

Kyle considered the guys standing near him dressed in work clothes or suits, their ties loosened, and he wondered about their stories. He wished he had his camera. The stories behind these people would be fascinating, yet they all came here for pretty much the same reason: companionship.

"I'm glad you didn't bring it."

Kyle looked up, puzzled.

"Your camera," Tony said placing a bottle of beer in front of him. "I know what you're thinking. I lived with you for four years." Shaking his head, he said, "They wouldn't appreciate having their pictures taken."

"I know, but the thought was tempting."

"Not in this bar." Tony said refilling the shot glass of the man sitting next to Kyle. Tony turned to Kyle and asked, "What's up?"

"You do know me well," Kyle said. "Here's the thing. I'm going to New York to pursue my career. I'm going to need to get a job in the evenings to support myself until I find my dream. I want you to teach me the basics of being a bartender."

"What about your experience working at old man Rappel's restaurant?"

"Most restaurants close way before midnight. I need a job that gives me late hours so I'm free during the day to find a job in my field."

"I guess that makes sense." Tony reached below the counter and pulled out a frayed copy of *The Bartender's Manual.* "Here," he said. "Study this. No, memorize it and then come back. I'll talk to the owner. Maybe he'll allow you to work with me for a while, although I doubt he'll pay you."

When Kyle looked at him with raised eyebrows Tony quickly added, "But you can keep your tips."

After he got home, Kyle fell onto his bed. Opening the manual he began to read:

Bartending Hygiene and Cleanliness.

Keep the bar organized and tidy.

Clean shakers and strainers after each use.

Wash and dry hands often.

Take care of your hands and keep nails trimmed short…

"Kyle," Joan stuck her head through the open door, "Lisa's downstairs." She stepped closer. "What are you reading?"

"A bar-tender's manual. Tony gave it to me."

She waited for further explanations and then she repeated, "Lisa is downstairs."

Kyle flung the book aside. "What does she want?"

"I don't know. Say hello maybe. She said she hasn't seen you since you got back from college."

"I've been busy."

"Well, you tell her that." Joan left the room, and he followed.

As soon as Lisa spotted him coming down the stairs, her eyes lit up and she walked toward him.

"Hi, Kyle. How are you?"

"Fine," he said and strolled past her. "What're you doing here?"

"I was in the neighborhood..." She blushed at the blatant lie. He looked at her face and saw the tears surging in her eyes. *Damn, he didn't feel like dealing with her today.* He seldom returned her phone calls and tried everything he could to avoid her. He knew how she felt about him, but he had never encouraged her in any way. Once or twice, he had considered taking advantage of her, but he dismissed the thought of seducing her. She was a nice girl, and besides, he had plans. He wanted only friendship, and he could do without that.

"What have you been doing since you got back from college?" she asked.

"Looking for a job, like everyone else. I heard you're working. Do you like the job?"

"Yes, very much. I'm planning to go to night school in the fall to get my MA in child care. I love working with children."

"Good for you. I hate being around a bunch of screaming brats."

She closed her eyes. Two spots of color flared on her cheekbones. "I've been invited to a birthday party at my friend Lynn's this Saturday and wondered if you want to go with me."

He turned his head and rolled his eyes. "Sorry, I can't. I'll be working with Tony at the bar."

"At the bar?"

"Yeah, the Iron Fist Tavern."

"I thought you wanted a career in photojournalism?"

"I do, but until then I've got to earn some money." He ran his fingers through his hair. Fighting his impatience, he said, "Look, I'll be busy every night, and in between I must study about a zillion combinations of cocktails. The list is so long, it makes my head spin. So if you'll excuse me," he opened the door. "Thanks for coming. See you around."

She looked at him with sad eyes and walked past him without saying a word. He stared after her as she approached her car, her shoulders slumped.

"Why did you have to be so mean to her?" Joan stood in the kitchen doorway.

Kyle slammed the door shut. "Is she dense or what? How do I make her understand I'm not interested in a romantic relationship?"

"She's a real nice girl..."

"Yes, I know." He scowled and repeated. "I know she's a nice girl, and I like her, but that's all. By the way, I got a call from the editor at the *Register*. They hired me as a stringer. I've got an assignment on Friday covering the Daughters of the American Revolution luncheon." He wrinkled his nose.

Joan frowned, and he fell into laughter. "I'm kidding, Mom. Don't be so serious. I'm glad for the opportunity, really."

"And you'll do a good job. They're going to discover you've got talent."

He put his arm around her. "I hope so."

The next evening Kyle reported for work at the Iron Fist Tavern, bartender's manual in hand. Tony handed him an apron and inspected his hands.

"Don't worry, I washed them three times," Kyle growled.

"Good. Remember to keep washing them during the course of the night." Tony took the manual from him and placed it beneath the counter. "Don't let any of our patrons see you looking up things. It'll ruin our reputation. If you're in a bind, ask me. Now get to work; we've got customers." He sent Kyle to the other end of the bar where two men wearing dark green, cotton work clothes stood. As he walked toward them, one of the men called out to him, "Two drafts."

"Coming up." Kyle sighed with relief.

CHAPTER 4

———————

THE SUMMER PASSED QUICKLY AND by the end of August Kyle served drinks on demand without ever having to refer to the manual again. More importantly, he had acquired an education in people skills that would benefit him throughout the rest of his life. People frequented the bar for many reasons. It was a place where they met friends and co-workers, felt comfortable, and were accepted. Realizing for the first time the loneliness dominating so many people's lives, Kyle became a skilled, but detached listener. He recorded many stories on his computer. Only the photos were missing. And great photos they would have been: The bricklayer, in his sixties, who won $40,000.00 in the lottery. He stormed in one evening waving his ticket. "All drinks on me," he announced, and Tony and Kyle poured without stopping. When it came time to pay the bill, the man, who at this point was quite drunk said, "I have to cash in my ticket before I can pay you guys." He wrote an IOU and left the bar singing loudly. He was never seen again and the owner of the Iron Fist Tavern made Tony and Kyle pay for the tab.

September 1, he said goodbye to Tony and his friends at the bar. He packed his suitcase while Joan watched with tearful eyes. They drove to the bus station in Kyle's car, where he hugged Joan and Luke, and promised to return for a visit soon.

Luke had already begun classes at the local community college and needed transportation. Before boarding the bus, Kyle handed him the car keys. "Here, little brother," he said. "She's yours for good."

"All right!" Luke's fingers curled around the key. When he'd heard his mom and Kyle discuss the folly of owning a car in New York City, his heart began to beat faster, and he assumed the Chevy would become his. But when Kyle later considered having Joe sell the vehicle because he needed the money, Luke's spirits dropped. Now the car was his, and he was eager to take it for a spin.

Kyle boarded the bus. "Bye, I'll call once I get settled."

Luke glanced at his Mom. Tears streamed down her face. He took her hand and squeezed it. "He'll be fine, Mom. No need to worry about him."

"I know."

The bus left the parking lot and Joan and Luke waved with both hands. Joan stood still until the bus was out of sight. Then Luke nudged her. "Let's go, Mom." He walked away and she followed reluctantly. He climbed into the driver's seat of Kyle's Chevy and reached across the passenger seat to open the door for Joan and she got into the car.

When they arrived home, Luke spotted Lisa on the front porch. "What's she doing here?"

"I don't know, honey, but you go into the house and give me a chance to speak to her privately," Joan said as she exited the car.

"Okay." Bolting up the porch steps, Luke lingered for a second. "Hi. Lisa." He noticed her red-rimmed eyes and frowned. He believed her tears to be wasted. He always thought her to be stunning and had a crush on her ever since he was twelve. Kyle was such a fool to push her aside, but then maybe with Kyle out of the picture, he stood a chance with her. Joan gave a low cough as she approached, and Luke hurried into the house. "See you later, Lisa." She didn't reply. Joan sat down next to her and put her arm around Lisa, which prompted a flood of tears.

"He didn't even say good-bye to me," Lisa said as she blew her nose. "I thought we were friends. I love him so much. Why can't he see that?" She dropped her head on Joan's shoulder.

"I know, I know." Joan gently pushed Lisa back. She took her hands and said, "Look, Lisa, I know Kyle thinks the world of you, and he loves you too, just not the way you want him to. He's got a lot of growing up to do. There is no room for a relationship in his life right now. You must forget about him."

Lisa shook her head. "I can't."

"Yes, you can. In time, you'll meet a nice young man who will love you and appreciate you, trust me."

Inside the house, behind the closed front door Luke stood listening. *Yes, and I'll be that guy. Kyle is a fool to turn his back on you, Lisa, but not me. I'll make you forget that louse. I'll never hurt you like that.* He must plan his strategy. Turning, his eyes darkened with determination, he mounted the stairs taking long strides.

CHAPTER 5

———◆———

THE BUS RUMBLED DOWN THE road. The first stop was Portland. Stretched out on the backseat and napping, Kyle awoke when he noticed the smell. Ugly grey smoke emanated from behind the backrest of his seat. He bolted up and investigated. At this point, other passengers noticed the odor. Kyle hurried up front to warn the driver just as they entered the outskirts of Portland. The driver pulled into a strip mall parking lot and urged everyone to leave the bus immediately. The people disembarked in an orderly fashion and gathered at a safe distance away from the bus, while the bus driver opened the engine compartment door.

Approaching the passengers, he said, "I'm no mechanic, but this bus isn't safe to drive. I've got to call the office. They'll send another bus. In the meantime, I suggest you people hang around close by." He pointed to a coffee-shop. "Why don't you all wait in there, and I'll keep you posted." The group walked away chatting noisily. Kyle followed slowly. He passed a kiosk and stopped to buy a newspaper. Checking his watch, it showed 11:00 A.M., he pushed through the revolving door of the café. All seats appeared to be taken except for one empty chair at a small table occupied by a young woman. He glanced at her briefly and turned when she called out to him.

"You're welcome to join me if you like."

He hesitated as he weighed his options. She removed her purse from the chair and pushed it out. He looked at her, and she smiled. She was beautiful, her face, full and round and framed by honey-colored hair cut short. Her eyes reminded him of the color of dark rum. He walked toward her and sat down.

"Thanks. I appreciate your kindness," he said.

"Kindness has nothing to do with it," she replied with a gleam in her eye. "I'm bored. I've an appointment in about an hour from now, and I'm just passing time. Might as well spend it with you. Amy Sloan," she stretched out her hand.

"Kyle Weldon." He held her hand a bit longer than necessary and his eyes locked with hers. She blinked and reached for her coffee mug.

"So the bus broke down."

His eyebrows rose, and she laughed. "I saw the smoke." She pointed her head in the direction of the stranded bus. "Where are you from?"

"Graceville, heading for New York City." He paused and then said sheepishly, "New York City or Bust."

"Come again?"

"Well, when the pioneers headed west in the 1800's looking for a better life, they put the phrase *California or Bust* on the doors of their properties. That's kind of my situation. I am heading for New York to find a job."

"So you're a photographer," she pointed to the camera dangling from his wrist.

"I have a degree in photojournalism. Fresh out of college. Spent the summer working with my buddy Tony at a local bar mastering the skill of bar tending, which I hope will subsidize my expenses while I look for a day job."

"You like to take pictures."

"Yep, I have taken pictures since I can remember. My dad gave me my first camera when I turned seven. In college, I worked for the newspaper and in between got a story or two published in national magazines." He turned to the waitress, "Coffee please."

"But why New York? There are many opportunities right here in Portland. Have you thought about applying at *The Portland Journal?*"

"Frankly, no. I don't want to be stuck at a place where there's no opportunity to move ahead."

She studied him quietly. *He may have potential and the looks to go with it. Inexperienced and having small town written all over him, but if he **is** good, he could have a promising future.*

"May I see some of your work? Have you a portfolio?" she asked.

"Yes, but it's in my suitcase."

"Go get it," she demanded.

"Wait a minute. Why are you interested, you don't know me?"

"My dad owns *The Portland Journal.* I guarantee if I approve of your portfolio he'll agree to see you, and the rest will be up to you." She shot to her feet, threw a ten- dollar bill on the table, and grabbed her bag. When he remained seated, she said, "Are you coming?"

"Where are we going?"

"My apartment. I want to see your portfolio."

He began to laugh. "This is unreal," he said. "I'm being picked up by a beautiful woman…"

"Who is offering you the opportunity of a lifetime," she said as she moved closer, her body almost touching his. He could smell her perfume, and his senses began to reel.

"I don't need to pick up men, trust me," she said giving him a dazzling smile. Turning and walking away she glanced over her shoulder and saw him rise. He caught up with her as she left the café.

"I'll get my luggage," he said. He had made up his mind quickly. What did he have to lose? He could always catch another bus. He whistled as he approached the bus driver.

Amy proceeded toward her car while speaking briefly into her cell phone and got into her vehicle. She backed away from the curb and drove the late model Jaguar slowly toward the broken down bus. Seeing her approach, Kyle thanked the driver, and deposited his suitcase into the open trunk. He slammed it shut and slipped into the passenger seat.

"Nice car."

"Thanks," she said and pulled into the traffic.

CHAPTER 6

———◆———

AS THEY DROVE THROUGH THE business district of Portland, Kyle was amazed how seascapes and cityscapes blended harmoniously in the city, perched on a peninsula and jutting out into island-studded Casco Bay. He focused his camera.

"Portland represents a unique balance between architectural traditions of the past and modern architecture," Amy said. He kept taking pictures, and she continued. "The quality and style of architecture in Portland is in large part due to the succession of well-known 19th-century architects who worked in the city.

"The Great Fire of July 4, 1866, destroyed most of the commercial buildings in the city, half the churches, and hundreds of homes. After the fire, Portland was rebuilt with brick and took on a Victorian appearance. On your right is the Franklin Towers," she said. "It's a 16-story residential complex. At 175 feet, it is Portland's tallest building. You'll find nuggets of modern architecture squeezed between historic structures.

"You have to visit Fort Gorges. It's a small, deserted, never-used fort built around 1860 in the middle of the harbor, and every day with the tides, it seems to sink into the ocean and rise again. The roof is piled high with earthen ramparts, and in the spring the plants growing on top give the fort a funny look with its crown of green sprouting wildly. You'll be able to capture some great shots." She turned to him and smiled. The camera was pressed against his face.

They arrived at a building with its street facades composed entirely of lime-stone. Elements of Art Deco styling decorated the entry way. The structure used setbacks at the upper floors to create terraces for several apartments and provide visual interest from a distance.

Amy parked the car in the adjacent parking lot. Kyle retrieved his luggage and followed her as she headed toward the front door via a cobblestone path. They entered a large lobby across which Amy lead the way to the elevators and pushed the button.

"This looks like an old building, magnificent design…"

"But it has all the comforts of home," she interjected.

The bell chime announced the fifth floor. "That's us," Amy said, and they exited. She hunted for her key hidden in the depth of her huge purse, and stopped in front of apartment 505. She opened the door and motioned him to enter.

"Wow," was all he could say when he deposited his suitcase onto the floor. He stood in the living room of the apartment and looked around. The fundamental simplicity defined the temporary décor. The walls were splashed with a soft white, and complemented by a bright orange sofa and two black leather club chairs. Soft pillows in white, muted blue and red microfiber accented the furniture. A black coffee table held the latest copy of *Vogue* magazine. He walked over to the window which extended across the entire wall facing south. Below him Portland bustled with late morning traffic.

"Let me give you the grand tour." Amy led the way, and he followed. The white cabinets in the kitchen accented the pale green painted walls. All the appliances were stainless steel. "Here is the bedroom." She pushed open the door. The colossal room was bright and sunlit. Kyle's eyes fell on the king-size bed flanked by two mahogany night tables with stainless steel trim, and a large dresser of the same design. The second bedroom had been converted into an office furnished with an oversized desk, a filing cabinet, and a damask covered red futon. A large flat-screen TV hung on the wall facing the futon. "You're welcome to use my office. I have an excellent printer."

She shut the door, and they returned to the living room. "Do you like my apartment?"

"I've never seen anything quite like it." In his mind, pictures of the cottage by the sea with the comfortable cozy interior flashed by like a slide presentation. He stared at the black acrylic tables bordering the sofa. Large light bulbs attached to stainless steel extensions curved toward the sofa from both ends. He turned and spotted a sculpture shaped like a crooked wagon wheel sitting on a pedestal. He walked closer and studied the object, which was carved out of white marble.

"What's this?"

"Why it's a nude. This is a creation by Ramon Sciaffo, my favorite sculptor." She came closer, and her hand caressed the sculpture. "It's a reproduction. I can't afford his original." Her eyes flashed, and she said, "Someday I will. Someday I'll get all the things I want." She moved her body close to his, wrapped her arms around his neck, pulled his head down and kissed him on the mouth.

When she drew away, he placed his arms on her hips, held her at arm's length, and said, "What about my portfolio?"

She threw her head back and laughed. "Yes, but first things first," she said as she took his hand and moved toward the bedroom. "We've got lots of time for that."

"Whatever you say, lady," Kyle said and kicked the door shut.

"Where do you keep the cork screw?" Kyle shouted from the kitchen. When she didn't answer, he carried the wine bottle into the bedroom. Amy sat naked on the bed, her legs curled beneath her studying the photos spread out in front of her. Her long slender neck with skin smooth as silk begged to be kissed. He looked at her small, firm breasts and a dizzying current raced through him. She was utter perfection.

Amy looked up. "These are good, Kyle. You have a keen eye." She scrunched her forehead. "Yes, Dad must take a look at these," she murmured and rose from the bed. As Kyle took in her nude body, his pulse began to rise. He dropped the bottle onto the fake tiger rug lining the side of the bed and reached for her. She snuggled up to him and whispered in his ear, "As a matter of fact, you are a man of many talents."

The sun was high in the sky when Kyle woke up. He reached over and found the other side of the bed empty. He sat up and looked around. The place was a mess. Half-filled wineglasses on the night table, the empty bottle on the floor next to the corkscrew, and his clothes strewn all over the place. A note taped to the bedroom door caught his eye. He jumped out of bed and crossed the room. Removing the note, he read: *I'm sorry I had to leave. I'm a working girl, you know. I made an appointment with Dad for you. Be there at 11:00 A.M. sharp. He doesn't like to be kept waiting. See you tonight.* She listed the address and ended the note with a bright pink imprint of her lips. Kyle smiled and kissed it. They had made love all night long. She seemed insatiable. Pictures of their passion flashed in front of him. *Amy, you're something else.*

"Taxi," the doorman flagged down a cab. Kyle tipped him and climbed into the back seat. He gave the driver the address and leaned back in the seat, clutching his portfolio. His hands were cold, but beads of perspiration gathered on his forehead. He realized he was more nervous than he cared to admit. Landing a job with the paper could provide him with great opportunities. Unlike Graceville, Portland was a large city, and it could be a stepping stone that eventually propelled him to New York City, where he really wanted to work. Amy had said her dad was outrageously demanding; that's why she would never work for him. Three years older than Kyle, she had been working for a brokerage house for three years, and had already moved up within the company. He didn't know how much money she was making, but judging by her apartment and the car she drove, he guessed she was doing quite well.

The cab came to a halt, and Kyle reached for his wallet. They had arrived at a 19th century cast-iron-front building in the heart of Portland. The sign above the revolving glass doors read *The Portland Journal.* Kyle climbed out of the taxi, and the driver took off. He stood still, looking up at the huge gold-leaf letters, when a young woman bumped into him. "You're blocking the door," she said and pushed past him.

"Sorry," he called out to her, but she was gone. He took a deep breath and proceeded through the door. He stopped at the information desk. "Third floor. Mr. Sloan is expecting you," he was told by a young man impeccably dressed. He decided to take the stairs and arrived a little breathless on the third floor. A receptionist asked him to follow her. They walked down a long carpeted hallway lined with doors until she stopped and knocked on one.

"Come in." The voice resonated from within.

She opened the door and motioned Kyle to enter and have a seat in front of the desk. A man was sitting with his back to him, facing a window while talking on the phone. He quickly hung up and turned. Kyle looked at him and his face brightened.

"Kyle," the man said and rose. "How nice to see you again. Richard Sloan." He stretched out his hand. "How is the old Chevy running?"

"Why it's you...," he stuttered but regained his composure quickly. "Very nice to meet you Mr. Sloan."

Richard Sloan sat down and leaned back in his chair. "Let's see how long has it been? Four years I believe."

"That's correct," Kyle replied. "I have never had a chance to properly thank you for funding the repair of my car. It meant a lot to me."

"Well, it was my pleasure. You did me a great service that night. Believe me, there were several people on the road that night that passed without stopping to lend a hand. When Amy phoned me and gave me your name, I was pleasantly surprised and looked forward to seeing you again."

Kyle nodded while his heart thumped. Did Mr. Sloan just want to reminisce and then send him on his way?

"Well, let me see your portfolio," he said, and Kyle eagerly handed him the folder.

"So you are a photojournalist," Mr. Sloan said. "Amy told me the photos were quite good, and I trust her judgment on that topic." He leafed through the pages while Kyle sat on the edge of the seat, his hands clasped tightly. Besides Amy and now Mr. Sloan, the only person who had ever seen his portfolio was his mom and she raved about it. He expected that kind of reaction from her but this man was a stranger, who looked at his work objectively. Having Mr. Sloan view his portfolio, was a true test. *If Mr. Sloan likes my work, it may open some doors for me, he nixes it…well, I'm not even going to think that way.*

The silence in the room was intimidating; the only sound noticeable was the steady ticking of an antique schoolhouse clock decorating the wall above a sideboard stacked with framed photographs.

At last Richard Sloan closed the portfolio, removed his glasses, and sat back in his chair. He looked at Kyle and said, "There are some excellent shots in here." He leaned forward. "As you know, photojournalists report what they see compared to traditional reporters who write stories. A photojournalist uses photographs instead of words which makes the task more difficult. There are three principles that apply to photojournalism: timeliness, objectivity and narrative."

Kyle listened intensely.

"Excelling in capturing day-to-day events and reporting them via pictures," Richard Sloan continued, "is what photojournalism is all about. Objectivity, the second principle, means the subject matter must be presented in an honest and unbiased way. In your narrative, your images must gel with other news elements so that the facts may be understood by viewers within a cultural framework. I guess you know all this by now. If you haven't already, I advise you to lock these three principles inside your head and never forget them. Reiterating them out loud must be the first thing you do in the morning and the last thing at night when you recite your prayers. Do you pray, Kyle?" Richard Sloan said and chuckled.

Kyle shook his head. He hadn't prayed in years. Since his father's death, he had struck God from his life. Deep down, he believed himself to be an atheist. There was one chance for human beings, and that was right here in this far-from-perfect world. "I don't believe in prayer," he said.

"Well, that is your business. Any questions?"

"Does that mean I've got the job?"

"Yes, but let me explain how we do things around here. You'll be working free-lance. We pay for each job you turn in. We'll send you on assignments, but you are free to work for other venues as well. How does that sound to you?"

"Perfect." Kyle's mind was spinning. *I got the job. This man believes in me; he likes my photographs.*

As if Richard Sloan had read his mind, he now said, "I think you have talent, Kyle, but make no mistake, there's a lot to learn and don't be discouraged when our editors reject some of your work." He picked up the phone. "Conley, what projects do you have coming up?" Richard Sloan listened quietly, nodding his head occasionally. "Sounds good. I've got someone here who has joined our team. Any of the subjects you mentioned will do. I'm sending him down." He hung up and rose from his chair. He walked around the desk and stretched out his hand. "Welcome to our staff, Kyle. Good luck. Work hard and you'll move ahead. If you have any problems, Conley will help you as much as he can. He's a good guy. Has been with me for three decades."

Kyle shook his hand. "Thank you, Mr. Sloan, for giving me this opportunity. You won't be disappointed."

Richard Sloan walked him to the door, and opened it, and pointed toward the hallway. "Five doors down, on the left. Conley's waiting for you." He gave Kyle an encouraging smile, stepped back inside his office and shut the door.

Kyle proceeded quietly on the carpeted floor. He stopped when he saw the sign, Conley Brown, Editor. He knocked on the door. "Come in," a soft voice with a slight southern drawl replied. He entered and approached the desk. A middle aged woman leaned over a computer, her fingers flying across the keyboard. She looked up. "Howdy." She pointed to the glass door and yelled, "Conley, Mr. Weldon is here." Turning to Kyle she smiled and said, "Go ahead; he won't bite."

"Thanks." Kyle pushed through the door.

Conley Brown, a short, stocky man, a Danny DeVito-lookalike with an extra decade and an impish smile, walked toward him. His wire rimmed glasses sat on the top of his head. "Hello, Kyle. Have a seat." He reached for the portfolio clammed underneath Kyle's arm. "Let me see this." He glanced through it briefly and handed it back to Kyle. Without commenting on it, he said, "Your assignment is covering the new war memorial to be unveiled tomorrow. It is dedicated to five Portland residents who fought and disappeared during the war in French Indo-China."

"Vietnam," Kyle mused.

"Yes. The memorial is located at South State Park. I need pictures plus a brief story. We don't want a lot of details on the five guys. They're local heroes. The event takes place at 11:00 A.M. Any questions?"

Kyle shook his head.

"Good. On your way out, stop at Nikki's desk and she'll see to it you get a press pass."

"Thank you, sir." Kyle shook his hand, "I appreciate this opportunity. I'll try not to disappoint you."

"I'm counting on it," Conley said his lips curving into a vague smile.

Kyle left the room. Nikki handed him several forms to fill out. "This will get you on the payroll," she said. "After you're finished here stop on the second floor. See the woman at the glass-walled workstation and she'll arrange for your press pass."

CHAPTER 7

———◆———

"ANYONE HOME?" AMY STOOD IN the living room, kicking off her shoes and dropping her briefcase onto the floor. "Kyle, where are you?"

"Right here." He emerged from the kitchen with a towel wrapped around his waist carrying a steaming casserole. He placed it onto the dining room table. Amy's eyes followed him in amazement. The table was set for two, tapered candles lit up the area, and the filled wineglasses reflected the glittering light.

"Hey, what's going on…" before she could finish he had taken her into his arms and kissed her passionately. He finally let her go.

"I see," she threw her head back and laughed heartily. "You got good news today, didn't you?" She untangled from his arms and walked over to the table. "This lasagna looks delicious. I'm famished."

The timer went off in the kitchen, and Kyle hurried away from her. He returned with a basket filled with buttery garlic bread and a bowl of tossed salad. "Voila, Mademoiselle! Dinner is served."

"You are full of surprises. I know you have many qualities," she said and gave him a wink, "but I'd never have guessed cooking is one of them."

They sat down. She unfolded her napkin and inhaled deeply. "I love lasagna, but where did you learn to cook?"

"I don't know how to cook."

"Oh, I see, this is store-bought" She filled her plate and took a mouthful. "Delicious," she said. "Tell me, how did it go with Dad?"

Kyle told her of the meeting and his first assignment. "I had met your dad years ago. It was quite uncanny seeing him again." Amy stared at him in surprise, and he continued. "He had a flat tire late at night while traveling outside of Graceville. I changed the tire for him, and he anonymously paid to have my old Chevy repaired."

"That's Dad. He's a generous man, hardworking and principled, unlike his daughter," she said with a sneer. The remark was lost on Kyle who was sipping his wine. "You work hard," she continued, looking at him furtively, "and he'll treat you right."

"That's the impression I got." He turned to her. "I don't know how to thank you, Amy."

"Oh, I can think of a way," she said and pushed her chair back. Unzipping her skirt, she headed for the bedroom. "Are you coming?"

"Right behind you," he said as he caught up with her and threw her over his shoulder while she giggled and kicked her feet.

Kyle cleaned off the dining room table. The clock struck 2:00 A.M. as he padded around naked in the kitchen filling the dishwasher.

"Why didn't you wake me?" Wearing Kyle's shirt, Amy stood in the doorway. Her sensuous beauty struck him like thunderbolts. Things were happening too fast. He didn't want to get involved in a relationship, opting to concentrate on a career instead; however, the depth of his passion for her stunned him. He knew he had never felt this way about any woman.

"I woke up and couldn't go back to sleep, so I decided to do something useful." He kissed her on the top of her head. "Go back to bed," he said. "I'm almost done here. Tomorrow I'll look for a place to live. I have some money to tide me over until I get paid. I also need a job."

"But you have a job now."

"I get paid on a commission basis. I need a steady income. I'll check out the local pubs. I'm an experienced bartender."

"Tending bar and have all the women drooling over you," she exclaimed. "I won't have it. Look," she said and put her arm around his shoulder, "why don't you stay here? I've got lots of room, and you can use your time between assignments to polish up your craft. What do you say?"

He hesitated.

"I won't have it any other way. It's settled."

"Maybe I can help pay the rent?"

"I own this place. There's no rent to pay. When Mom died, she left me enough money to buy this condo and then some."

"I'm sorry to hear about your mom," he said and paused. "Okay, but I buy the groceries. Deal?"

She didn't answer; instead she drew him close. ·

CHAPTER 8

———

WHEN KYLE ARRIVED AT SOUTH Park a small crowd of protesters surrounded the new war memorial chanting, "Remember the Dead." Drizzling rain accompanied by a chill in the air caused the temperature to drop and Kyle to zip up his jacket after he got out of the cab. He studied the obelisk-shaped, gray granite slab featuring the carved kneeling shape of an emaciated prisoner in shackles. The inscription read: *We never forget our heroes - The Vietnam War – 1959-1975.* The five names of the missing men were listed below. Kyle moved in to take a photo when one of the protesters bumped into him. Kyle turned and asked, "Why are you protesting?" The man hesitated, and Kyle pulled out his pad.

The man finally said, "We want the names of all the missing and dead listed."

Kyle said, "But this monument is specifically dedicated to five local men..."

"I live in Vermont," the man interrupted. "I lost my father in that war. Hugo here," he pointed to the man next to him, "lost two brothers. Singling out five men ain't fair."

"But there are memorials all over the United States dedicated to war veterans."

"Well, there ain't any in Maine," the man said and pushed Kyle aside as he joined the others in their chanting.

"Hey, you're a reporter?" a woman addressed Kyle. "Make sure you're getting your story right," she threatened.

"I'm a photojournalist. May I ask why you're protesting?"

"I lost my husband in that war," she said. "His body was never found – missing in action, they said. I still keep hopin' against hope that he'll come back to me."

"Do you live in Portland?"

"Obviously not," she cackled, "or his name would've been listed. I live in Bangor."

Kyle had stepped back to take a photo of the crowd as they circled the monument when he heard shouting. Not far from him, two men argued, their voices raised, their fists thrown into the air. Before he could duck, Kyle was shoved to the ground his camera clutched firmly to his chest. He dropped his note pad. Someone stepped on his foot as he scrambled to get up. People screamed and exchanged blows. Kyle managed to retreat safely from the havoc and kept snapping photos. The sirens, first muted but becoming loud and shrill, announced the police had arrived. The protesters took off in every direction.

"Come," a young man grabbed Kyle's elbow and dragged him away. "You don't want to be here when the cops come." They hurried across South Park, and when the man spotted a café he pulled Kyle inside.

"How about a cup of coffee," he said, "while this commotion simmers down?"

Catching his breath, Kyle said, "Fine with me."

The sat at one of the tables and gave the waitress their order.

"Tell me," Kyle said, "what happened just now? By the way, I'm Kyle and you are…"

"You don't need to know my name. I live in New Hampshire."

"Then what are you doing here in Maine, protesting this event?"

"I was hired." The man leaned back and laughed. "You might say I'm a professional protester." He stroked his chin, and his coal black eyes twinkled as he looked at Kyle.

"Do you mind if I quote you in my article?"

"Nope." He smirked. "Ask me any questions you like," the man added.

"Who hired you?"

"Have no idea. Some woman approached me on campus. Said she'd pay me a hundred bucks for heckling a politician during a campus speech. She took my name and phone number. Me and a lot of other people. She calls quite often. She pays traveling expenses if I have to go to another state."

Kyle kept scribbling on his pad. "How do you get paid?"

"Always cash and in person."

"You mean she is here?"

"She was here." He finished his coffee. "Here and gone." He rose and stretched out his hand. Nice talking with you. "I gotta go. Heading for Albany."

"Another protest?"

"Yep. Quote me on anything I said, but no pictures." He left the café.

"Would you like anything else, sir?" The waitress asked.

Kyle's head shot up. He was polishing up his notes and had totally forgotten his surroundings.

"No thanks," he said. She handed him the check. "Come back and see us again." She gave him a flirty smile, which he ignored. He dropped the money onto the table and left. When he stepped outside, he noticed except for a few people strolling past the monument, South Park was deserted. He decided to save cab fare and walked back to Amy's apartment. He inserted the memory card into his computer and studied the photos. Then he hooked up to Amy's printer and ran copies.

Early the next morning, he finished up his report and left to turn it in. He arrived at the paper but never got past Nikki. "Conley is busy," she said and took the envelope from him. "How did it go yesterday?"

"Okay."

She handed him a paper. "Your next assignment."

He took it eagerly. "Thanks."

"Don't thank me yet."

He looked at the topic and frowned as he read: Homeless People in Portland, Maine.

"Are there many homeless in the city?" he asked.

She nodded. "You'd be surprised. Conley and Mr. Sloan have been working for years to bring the situation to the politicians' attention." She shrugged and continued, "It's not a popular topic." The phone rang. She picked it up and waved goodbye to Kyle, and he left the office.

"I'm home." Amy entered the apartment carrying a plastic bag. Kyle jumped up, ran toward her, and gave her a bear hug. Her purse and the bag she was carrying fell to the floor.

She squealed. "What a welcome."

He held her close and kissed her. When he finally let her go, she inhaled deeply. "You take my breath away," she said, "and I love it."

Kyle picked up her purse and the bag. He looked inside. "Subs," he said and looked at his watch. "I just realized what time it is. I'm starved." He rushed over to the table and proceeded to remove several volumes of books.

"What are you doing?" Amy said.

"I have a new assignment. I went to the library to educate myself on the plight of the homeless in Portland."

"The homeless?"

"Yes. I turned in my report on the memorial protest, and Conley assigned me a new project before he even had a chance to look at my work."

"I'm sure you did a great job," Amy said and poured the Chardonnay into two Waterford Crystal wine glasses.

They sat and munched on their food. Kyle lifted his glass and said, "Here's to the most wonderful woman I've ever met."

Amy raised hers and gazed at him tenderly.

"Amy, I think I've fallen in love with you," he said.

Her eyes moved away from his face, and she didn't answer.

"I know this is totally unexpected and probably an inconvenient time..."

"Kyle," she interrupted. "Don't confuse passion with love. Let's just have a good time and not worry about the consequences of the words 'I love you.'"

She saw his body stiffen and added quickly, "We know so little about one another. Before we make any declarations we may later regret, let's just enjoy each other to the fullest. What do you say?"

He lowered his head.

She studied his face surreptitiously. He was just a boy although he was energetic in bed. His passions met hers every time, but it was inevitable she would tire of him. She always did. There have been many men in her life. None of them had been able to harness her restless spirit. She glanced at him from beneath lowered lids. *Maybe he'll surprise me. It would be a welcome change, settle down, have a family. It's what Dad wants but is it the right thing for me?*

CHAPTER 9

———◆———

THE NEXT MORNING KYLE, TOOK the bus. He got off at Walton Street and walked past the boarded-up row houses. A man of undeterminable age sat on one of the front steps. He wore a torn Patriots sweatshirt, the hood tightly drawn over his head. An unkempt salt and pepper beard reached below his neck down where the broken zipper allowed the shirt to gape revealing a dirty-white undershirt. His pants hung loosely on his legs and reached to the sidewalk gathering on top of his filthy Converse sneakers.

"Good morning," Kyle said. The man looked at him suspiciously.

"It would be a good morning if I had a cigarette."

Kyle smiled and reached inside his pocket. He didn't smoke but had on impulse bought Marlboros yesterday; he silently thanked himself for paying attention to this instinct. He opened the pack, flipped up a cigarette and offered it to the man. The entire pack was snatched from his hand. The man pulled out matches and lit one. He inhaled deeply as he fingered the pack reluctant to return it to Kyle.

"Keep it," Kyle said.

"Much obliged." The cigarettes disappeared inside the pocket of the hoodie. For the first time, the man looked up at Kyle. He had bright blue eyes and pallid skin. His crooked smile revealed two missing upper front teeth.

"Well," he said, "obviously you want something. Go ahead, ask."

"You're correct." Kyle sat down next to him.

"You a reporter or something? They come down here all the time to ask questions. Always the same questions." He blew out a puff of smoke.

"My name is Kyle Weldon. I'm a photojournalist doing a piece on homelessness in the city for *The Portland Journal.*"

"You wanna take my picture? Go ahead, but it's going to cost you."

"How much?"

"Five bucks a pic."

Kyle nodded, reached inside his pocket, and handed the man a ten.

He snatched the bill from Kyle's hand and said "You have to forgive me for not being able to change into my good clothes. These are all I've got." He took a last long drag on the cigarette stub and flicked it out into the street. Leaning back, he said, "Shoot," and grinned widely.

"Later," Kyle said. "Let's talk first. Have you had breakfast?"

The man's eyes lit up.

"I see." Kyle said and rose. He waited for the man to get up. "Well, lead the way. I'm new to Portland. Breakfast is on me."

"All I can eat?"

"Of course."

"There's a diner about a block down the street." The man jumped up and began to walk. Kyle caught up with him.

They walked in silence and arrived at a small eatery. The man entered followed by Kyle. A scent of fresh brewed coffee and fried bacon filled the air.

"Mornin', Neill," the man said cheerfully.

"Hi there, Eddie." Neill, the owner, stood behind the counter. He turned, pulled a large paper cup from the shelf above him, and proceeded to fill it with coffee but Eddie stopped him.

"Not today, buddy." He pointed to Kyle and said, "This here is my new friend, Kyle. He's gonna buy me breakfast today." He winked at Neill and sat down at one of the small tables. Kyle nodded to Neill and joined Eddie.

"Neill is an all right guy. He gives me free coffee every day. In turn, I keep an eye on this place when he's closed for the night. This ain't the best of neighborhoods." Brushing his hair aside, he leaned, squinted, and assessed Kyle with a critical eye.

Kyle laughed. "I know what you're thinking, and you're wrong."

A stout woman in her forties approached to take their order. "What'll be, gents?" she asked.

"Breakfast, the whole works with double everything, bacon, eggs, toast."

"You keep this up you're gonna get fat. Eddie." She turned to Kyle. "And you, sir, do you want the same?"

"Lord no," Kyle laughed heartily. "Coffee and a bagel for me."

After they finished eating, Kyle pulled out his notepad. "So, what's your story?"

Eddie blinked. "My story? It'll bore you to death."

"Don't play games, Eddie."

Eddie wiped his face with the paper napkin and threw it on the plate. "I'm ready for a nap now."

Kyle stared at him intensely.

"What you gonna do if I tell you I don't feel like talking to you?" He rose. "I'm leaving now, and there's nothing you can do about it."

Kyle took a sip of his coffee. "You're not going to leave."

Eddie hesitated and then dropped onto his chair. "Yeah, I'll stay. Go ahead, ask your questions." He wiped his mouth and added, "I don't like thinking about the past." He lit a cigarette and watched the smoke curling into the air. "I like you, Kyle," he finally said, "but my story is dull and boring. There are millions of people like me."

"Let me be the judge of that. How old are you, Eddie?"

"Thirty-two."

Kyle's first reaction was shock. He guessed Eddie was close to forty-five, but then a shave and haircut would make a big difference. "Are you healthy?"

"Physically."

Kyle remained quiet.

"I used to be a truck driver based in Montpellier, VT. I owned my own rig. One day, I picked up a hitchhiker. He was just a kid. His car broke down on the highway, a hoax, which I later discovered."

"Where'd this happen?"

"North Carolina. He wanted to go to Virginia where he had family who would help him get his car. He was carrying a back-pack and a suitcase. I felt sorry for the kid." Eddie gave Kyle a smirk, and continued, "When I crossed into Virginia, I pulled into one of the truck stops. He jumped out of the truck wearing his backpack, and then reached for the suitcase."

"I said, 'Hey, no need for that. No one will bother your stuff here. I'll lock the doors if that'll make you feel better.' I could tell he had a hard time being parted from his suitcase, which made me a little suspicious. I got out of the cab and walked around the truck. When I got to the passenger side, the kid was gone. I figured he went to the john. I didn't see him there, though, and when I returned to the rig, he was nowhere in sight. I walked around looking for him, but gave up. It was getting dark, and I had to move on. I pulled out on the highway. I had forgotten all about the suitcase." Eddie paused and lit another cigarette offering one to Kyle, who shook his head.

"Yeah, I forgot. You don't smoke." He inhaled deeply and continued. "Anyway when I got home a day later, I spotted the suitcase and opened it. That's when I discovered the kilo of grass." Eddie shook his head, "And then I made the biggest mistake in my life. I called the police." He paused.

"You did the right thing."

"Did I? Well, let me tell you what happened." He threw his head back and laughed sarcastically while Kyle watched him quietly.

"They didn't believe a word I said. I got accused of dealing and spent five years of a ten-year sentence in the pokey. I lost everything, my rig, my license. When I got out I couldn't find a job. Nobody wants to hire an ex-con. I was innocent." He spat the words.

Kyle sat, stunned. He had never met anyone who'd been in prison. To have been falsely accused and serve time…he couldn't imagine the agony of this injustice.

"I've been homeless ever since," Eddie continued. "It's not such a bad life. There are a lot of good people who take pity on you and slip you a few bucks or treat you to a meal, like you did." He gave him a crooked grin. "But there are times when I have been beaten up, left for dead, and ended up in a hospital." He took one dirty finger and tapped it on Kyle's notepad. "That's what I want you to write." His voice rose with passion. "Write about the fact that I'm living in the gutter, going through people's trash to keep from being hungry while the other half lives like royalty."

"Who is the other half?"

"You and your cohorts at the paper where you work."

"I'm new at this job, but I understand that the paper has run many articles trying to draw the politicians' attention to the plight of the homeless…."

"Yeah, yeah," Eddie interrupted, "but nothing's being done." He rose. "Look," he said, "I've nothing against you. You've been swell. Thanks for the meal and the cigarettes, but I've got to go." He turned and took off. Kyle stared after him. He realized he didn't take one photo of Eddie. *I'll take some pictures of the area, the steps, where I first saw him. That'll do.*

Neill approached his table. "Eddie's story is gut-wrenching. He didn't tell you all of it. He was raped repeatedly in prison. Ended up in the hospital where they repaired his colon."

Raped? The poor guy. Kyle sat very still. He wasn't sure they had homeless people in Graceville. He'd never seen any.

"Eddie's a good guy, I wish I could help him more," Neill said.

Kyle looked up. "It looks to me like you're doing a lot already."

Neill grabbed the edge of the table and leaned closer to Kyle. "Look, you make damn sure you're getting everything in. Your article will be read by many people. Make it powerful. It must rattle our politicians who are blind to this problem. It only gets some attention during election time." He straightened up. "Breakfast's on the house." He walked away before Kyle could reply. "Just make damn sure you nail it all down," he said over his shoulder.

After Kyle left the diner, he snapped photos of the decaying neighborhood. He spotted Eddie in the distance sitting on the same steps. He zoomed in and clicked several times. His mind kept going back to Neill's words. *Politicians. I've never given them much thought. They have the power to make a difference, but only after pressure is put upon them? Aren't they elected by the people?* He sped up his pace. Eddie's story spun around in his head. *Maybe I can make a difference? My article must be short and to the point. The photos can make the story even more powerful.* He didn't want to waste time walking back to the apartment. He flagged a cab.

After he returned to the apartment, he opened his laptop and began to type. It was dusk when he stopped. The final draft was done. He wanted to go over it one more time. He rose and got a glass of water. On the way back from the kitchen, he remembered, *I've got to call Mom.*

Joan was finishing up the dishes when the phone rang.

"Kyle!" Her eyes lit up. "I'm so glad to hear from you. I was worried…"

"I know," he interrupted, "but there's no need. I'm a big boy now, remember?"

"Yes, yes, but tell me how you're really doing?"

He filled her in on everything except Amy. Somehow he couldn't bring himself to tell her.

"Where are you living? What's your address?"

"I have an apartment," he lied. "I'm living in Portland."

"Portland? I thought your destination was New York."

"That's a long story. We'll get into that later. I've got a job with *The Portland Journal.* I'm working on my second assignment."

She gasped, and when she spoke her voice had risen with excitement. "Kyle, I'm so proud of you. I wish your father could be here to share this wonderful news."

"I know. How is Luke? Is he taking good care of my car?"

"Yes, but it's his car now, remember?"

Kyle laughed. "Is he there?"

"No, dear, he went to a ball game."

"Well, got to go, Mom. I'll call again soon. Bye. Love ya." He hung up

"Me too. Bye," she said and then realized he didn't give her his address. *Strange. I guess he was too excited and just forgot.* She rose and put the last of the dishes away. *He sounds happy and seems to be doing well. I'll have to stop worrying about him.*

"Mom, I'm home." Luke entered the kitchen. "I'm hungry." He opened the refrigerator.

"There's some leftover apple pie," Joan said. "How was the game?"

"Fine. I saw Lisa there."

"How is she?"

"She had a little kid with her, about five years old. She said he comes to the day care where she works." He attacked the pie.

"Lisa cares about people. It's rare in a young person," Joan said.

I wish she cared about me. Out loud Luke said, "Yeah, she's nice. I like her."

CHAPTER 10

KYLE THREW HIS ARMS UP and stretched. He rose and flipped on a light. He checked his watch. *Where is Amy? She should have been home long before now.* He opened the fridge, reached for a can of soda, and walked out on the balcony. Dusk had veiled the city, and thousands of lights sparkled like lightning bugs.

The front door opened, and he jumped up. "Hey, I was worried about you." He drew her into his arms.

"Not now," she hiccupped.

He stepped back and took a closer look. Her cheeks were flushed and her eyes glazed. She had been drinking.

"Sorry I didn't call." She kicked her shoes off. "I had a meeting with a client. Verrrry important." She went into the bedroom and fell onto the bed. He followed.

"Amy," he said softly. She had passed out. He listened to her intermittent snoring, and heaved a sigh as he proceeded to undress her. Covering her with the blanket, he kissed her on the forehead. "Goodnight, my love," he said and walked out of the room, closing the door behind him.

"What's the matter? Do I have the plague or something?" Amy stood naked in the doorway. Stretched out on the couch, Kyle stirred. She approached and repeated the question. He opened his eyes and sat up slowly.

He ignored her question.

"You were feeling no pain last night. What happened?" he finally said.

She laughed. "Oh, Kyle, what an innocent you are." She walked over to him and sat on his lap.

"I'm waiting for an answer."

She snuggled up to him. "Well," she paused with meaning. "I had an important meeting with a client, and afterward he invited me to dinner. I didn't want to refuse. Business, you know. I can't be anti-social."

He looked incredulously at her, and before he could speak, she pulled him down on the floor. "You're so naive, Kyle. Maybe that's what makes you so damn attractive."

He tightened his arms around her, and his lips met hers.

The next morning, he printed his photos and made his selection. He checked his watch 9:30 A.M.

"Mornin'." Amy smiled uneasily as she stuck her head through the door. "Why didn't you wake me?"

"Aren't you old enough to know when it's time to get up and go to work?"

"Hmm," she said and paused while Kyle looked straight into her eyes. She blinked and turned. "I'll jump in the shower."

When she returned, wrapped in a towel, he was gone. *Well, aren't we petty? Got your feelings hurt, Kyle. Better get with it. You don't own me.* She pouted and dropped onto the couch. She liked the fact that he showed some backbone. Most of the guys she'd been with were wimps, spineless, unable to resist her manipulations. Those relationships never lasted long because she got bored quickly. *In many ways, you're still a kid, Kyle but you're learning fast.* She rose, poured herself a cup of coffee, and returned to the bedroom.

Kyler arrived at the paper. "Morning, Nikki. Is Conley in?"

"Go on in. He's expecting you."

Kyle gave a quick knock and entered. Conley looked up, pushed his glasses back on his head, and said without preamble, "There, take a look." He handed Kyle today's copy of *The Portland Journal*.

Kyle took the paper from him and read in amazement: Dedication of Viet Nam War Memorial Draws Heavy Protests. By Kyle Weldon. One photo showed the memorial and another the angry crowd surrounding the obelisk. He smiled as he studied the article.

Conley had been watching him and said, "Yeah, I know. It isn't on the front page. That doesn't mean it wasn't an excellent article. I like the photography. You've got potential."

"Thanks. I'm very pleased that my work made the paper." He handed him an envelope. "This is my homeless assignment."

"Great. I'll work on it today." Conley put the envelope on his desk. "How do you feel? You know, most budding photojournalists don't get their first assignment printed on page two. It usually gets buried on page 11 if it's not laughed out of the editor's office first." He pulled is glasses down. "I don't have anything for you today, but that doesn't mean you can't come up with a project of your own. Surprise me. In the meantime, I'll be in touch." He proceeded to open Kyle's envelope.

"Thanks." Kyle left the room. On his way back to the apartment, he stopped at a newsstand and picked up two copies of the paper. "I've got an article in here," he said to the vendor and pointed to page two.

"Sure you do," the man said and picked up the book he'd been reading.

Kyle laughed to himself. *I guess it is hard to believe.*

He stopped at the post office and mailed a copy to his mom. To save money, he walked back to the apartment. On the way he stopped at the photo studio he had passed so many times.

"Good morning," said a middle-aged man with unruly dark-brown hair and a purple birthmark on his right cheek as he approached Kyle. He wore a flowered vest over a white button-down shirt.

"Hi, I'm Kyle Weldon. I was wondering if I could look at some of the photographs on display in your gallery."

The man stretched out his hand. "Quentin Davis." They shook hands. "Kyle Weldon. Where have I heard that name?" The man said scratching his head.

Kyle extended the newspaper to him.

"Oh, that's you." He laughed. "I read the article this morning. The pictures are great. Are you disappointed because it didn't make page one?"

"A little. I guess I'm too impatient."

"Do you have a portfolio? I would like to see it. I often schedule exhibits for budding artists."

"Yes, I do. I'll drop it off." Kyle's breath came quickly.

He jogged back to Amy's apartment. *An exhibit! It's every photographer's dream.* He sped up his pace. *Things are happening pretty fast, and it is only because of Amy. I've been rude and insensitive. She works hard and having dinner with clients is part of her job. I can't be jealous. I must make it up to her.*

Half an hour later, he arrived at the apartment. He grabbed his portfolio but hesitated on the way out. He hurried into the kitchen and scribbled a note for Amy and put it onto the table. He checked the elevator but decided not to wait and use the stairs instead. While he hurried down the steps, Amy arrived on the fifth floor via the elevator.

"Kyle, I'm home," she called out cheerfully as she unlocked the apartment door. When she didn't get an answer, she checked all the rooms and ended up in the kitchen, where she found his note. She sat down and opened the newspaper she'd been carrying and began to read. Her cell phone rang.

"Yes," she said.

"Amy, have you seen today's paper?"

"Hi, Dad. Yes, I'm reading it right now."

"This was Kyle's first assignment. Conley just left my office. He showed me the new assignment Kyle turned in. I am impressed."

"I told you he had potential…"

"I know," he interrupted. "I want to talk to you about Kyle."

She frowned and put the paper down. "What about Kyle?"

"What are your plans regarding him?"

"Dad…"

"I know you're grown up and free to do as you wish, but based on your previous history with men…."

"Dad, I'm going to hang up. My life is my business. You can't squeeze me into a mold and have me act like a robot."

"I know, and if your mother was still alive…."

"Leave Mom out of this."

"Okay," he said, "But I like this young man, and I'm afraid he's not in your league. I don't want to see him crushed."

"Bye, Dad," she said and disconnected. *Crushed, he says. What about me?* She didn't know why she behaved this way. She was attracted to Kyle, and she knew she acted on impulse. He was already getting a little too possessive, but she wasn't ready to let him go.

The front door slammed. "Amy?"

"I'm in the bedroom, Kyle."

He rushed in to see her. His cheeks were flushed and his hair mussed. "You'll never guess what happened today."

He dropped on the bed, next to her and cupped her face. "Quentin Davis is thinking about doing an exhibit of my photos."

Her eyes grew wide. "Who is he? Wait a minute," she struggled to get free. "I remember the guy who owns the studio."

"Yes. I dropped off my portfolio today. He already told me he likes my pictures." He fell back on the bed. "God, Amy, do you know what that means?"

She leaned over him. "Oh, yes. Congratulations, Kyle."

"Thanks." He said and pulled her on top of him.

CHAPTER 11

———◆———

"HELLO."

There was silence on the other end of the line.

"Hello," Amy said impatiently.

"Excuse me, I must have the wrong number..." Joan hesitated and added, "I'm looking for Kyle Weldon."

"Just a minute." Amy turned. "Kyle," she called out and he appeared from the office. She handed him the phone.

"Yes," he said.

"Kyle, how are you?"

"Mom?" He swallowed deeply before he continued. "I'm doing great. How are you? How's Luke?"

"We're fine. We just got the newspaper you sent. Oh Kyle, we're so proud of you." Overcome with emotion Joan fought hard not to cry.

"Thanks, Mom. I'm very excited."

"...and happy?" She said.

He glanced at Amy. "Very happy, Mom."

Joan remained quiet for a moment, but he offered no further information. "That's good," she said. "Please keep in touch and remember, we love you. Bye, Kyle."

"Bye, Mom."

He hung up. She hadn't asked about Amy and he was relieved.

"Why didn't you tell her? She must be wondering who I am." Amy said with a smirk.

He missed it. He had walked over to the window.

"Kyle…"

He shot her a twisted smile and said, "I don't know. It wasn't the right time."

Joan sat quietly at her kitchen table. The phone conversation replayed in her mind over and over again. *A woman answered his phone. He must be staying with her. Kyle, what are you getting yourself into?* She shook her head. *He's a grown man, out on his own, making decisions, and I must let him go.* She rose with a sigh and went into the mudroom to check on her laundry.

◆

With the radio blaring through the open windows, Luke drove down Main Street. He'd just finished classes for the day and was bored. He turned into Acadia Avenue and slowed down when he reached Lisa's house. He had almost come to a stop and stretched his neck searching for any sign of her, when he heard shouting in back of him and a horn honking repeatedly. He quickly stepped on the gas and took off. As he looked through the rearview mirror, he spotted Lisa exiting the house and skipping down the steps. He put his foot on the brake, which elicited more yelling when the car in back of him swung around to pass.

"Are you crazy? You don't belong on the road, you maniac!" Laced with fury the voice rang in Luke's ears, and he kept his head turned into the opposite direction from the irate motorist. He backed up carefully this time and parked. Lisa stood on the sidewalk. She opened the mailbox and pulled out letters and circulars.

He jumped out of the car. "Hey, Lisa."

She looked up, surprised. "Luke," she said. "What are you doing here?"

He leaned against the mailbox crossing one leg over the other. "I just happen to be in the neighborhood when I saw you. It thought I'd stop and say howdy."

"Howdy?" Lisa said and laughed.

"Well, how are you? How's that?"

"I'm fine, Luke. By the way, how is Kyle?"

He shrank. The last thing he wanted to talk about was Kyle.

"Fine, just fine. Working in Portland at some newspaper. Look Lisa," he spoke fast not wanting her to interrupt, "do you want to go get a soda or a cup of coffee?

"With you?"

He frowned. "Yeah, with me. What's wrong with that?"

She looked him straight in the eyes, and he knew he finally had her attention.

"There's this quiet café on Walker Avenue…"

"Quiet?" She interrupted. She took his arm and pulled him over to the steps and sat down. When he remained standing, she pointed to the space next to her, and he dropped down.

"Look, Luke," she said slowly and deliberately. "You're a great kid…"

He opened his mouth but only shook his head when she continued. "I like you very much. After all, you're Kyle's brother. I see many similarities between the two of you. But if you have any intentions of hitting on me, you need to know I love Kyle with every fiber of my being. Always have, always will."

His jaw dropped as she continued. "In time he'll discover he loves me too." Her lips pressed tightly together she rose. "Bye, Luke."

"Hey, wait." He scrambled to his feet. "Look Lisa, you're wasting your time. Can't you give me a chance?"

"Luke, you should find someone your age. I'm sure there are lots of girls dying to go out with you."

"There are," he admitted freely, "but I don't want them. I want you."

"Sorry, Luke." She ran up the steps and waved. "See you around," she said and disappeared into the house.

He stared after her. *Well, that was quite clear. Now, I know how you really feel, Lisa, but don't worry. I'm not giving up. You'll change your mind in due time, I'll see to that.* He whistled as he walked to his car.

"Luke," Joan rushed from the kitchen. "Look at this." She handed him the newspaper with Kyle's article.

"Where's his picture?" Luke said.

"He took the photos, dear."

"No, I mean a picture of Kyle," he replied impatiently.

"He wrote the article and took the photos. Newspapers usually don't show photos of their photojournalists."

"That stinks. How's he ever going to become famous?"

"He's on his way to get some recognition, and…" She fell silent. Luke looked at her expectantly.

"I called Kyle today." Joan distractedly plucked at her cardigan. "He surprised me."

"How?" Luke moved closer to his mother. "Mom, what's up? You're acting strangely."

"A woman answered the phone when I called."

Luke's ears perked up. "A woman?" he said, "Why that's great."

Joan looked at him suspiciously. "What are you saying? He's not even been gone a month, and there's a woman in the picture already."

"What do you expect? Kyle isn't the celibate kind."

"Luke!" The rise in her voice surprised her.

Luke quickly put his arm around her. "Relax. I guess when he's ready, he'll let us know who this woman is." He brushed a kiss on her hair, left the kitchen, and raced up the stairs. *Kyle's with a woman. Swell! Now I must find a way for Lisa to find out*

CHAPTER 12

"KYLE, STOP BY AND SEE me this morning if you get a chance," Quentin said. "I'd like to discuss your portfolio."

"See you in a bit," Kyle replied and disconnected.

Kyle jogged the two miles to the studio. He hadn't been paid yet and was running out of money. His search for an evening job had been unsuccessful so far. Besides, Amy vehemently rejected the thought of Kyle tending bar.

He arrived a little out of breath. "Morning, Quentin."

"Hi, Kyle, follow me." He gestured for his assistant not to disturb them. They stepped into Quentin's office. "Have a seat." Seeing his portfolio was spread out on Quentin's desk, Kyle fought to conceal his anxiety.

"I've been looking these over," Quentin said. "You have talent. I'm especially impressed with your black and white photography." He picked up a photo taken during the protests at the Vietnam Memorial.

Kyle grinned from ear to ear and relaxed in the chair. "Thanks, that means a lot to me."

"I want to do an exhibit of your black and white photos."

Kyle opened his mouth, but words failed him.

"Well, what do you say?"

"I'm ecstatic and deeply honored that you think my work is good enough."

"My shows are well attended by people in the know. You'll earn rec-ognition. All photos on exhibit are offered for sale. Are you willing to part with some of them?" Quentin looked up.

Kyle gulped. "I could use the money."

"I thought so. So it's settled?"

"Yes. What do you want me to do?"

"Take more photos. Remember, black and white only. Oh, by the way, I take a 35% commission. We'll schedule the event for the end of November which will give us enough time to get everything lined up."

On his way back to the apartment, Kyle stopped to pick up a bottle of champagne. It made a huge dent in his vastly shrinking funds, but he expected to get paid for the two assignments he had completed for the Journal by the end of the week.

He rummaged through Amy's stuffed freezer and found two rib eye steaks. Expiration on the package dated a year ago. He sniffed the meat. Amy did little cooking but lots of shopping. He chuckled. *Wait until she hears my news. She'll be so proud of me. I owe her so much. She made it all happen.* He pulled out the small electric grill and checked his watch. She would be home around five. He had plenty of time. He took his camera, focused it on the Ramon Sciaffo sculpture, and took shots from several angles. He still considered the piece hideous, but decided to keep an open mind. He stepped out on the balcony. A flock of geese chatting noisily passed above him. He zoomed in and clicked in rapid succession. He dropped onto the comfortable wicker chair and put the camera down. His mouth curved into an unconscious smile. He'd never been so happy. Is that what being in love does to people? *And I know for certain I'm in love with Amy. I want to be with her all the time.*

"Hey, where are you?"

He hastened into the living room where she stood giving him a mocking frown. He swept her up and swung her around while she gig-gled and held onto him. When he finally put her down, she took his face between her hands and looked deeply into his eyes. "Let me guess. You got some good news today, right?"

"Fantastic news." He pulled her over to the couch. "Quentin is planning a show of my black and white photos. They will be available for sale."

"Really? Congratulations, Kyle. I knew your talent would be recognized." She said and hiccupped.

He looked at her suspiciously. "Have you been drinking?"

She shook her head and kissed him on the cheek. "I'm so happy for you." She handed him a small rectangular box tied with a purple ribbon.

"What's this?"

"A surprise," she said and smiled.

He tore at the ribbon, opened the box, and stared at a *Rolex* watch with a metal band. His eyes grew wide. "I can't accept this. This must have cost a fortune."

"This is a gift from me. Look at the back." The inscription read "To Kyle from Amy."

"I don't know what to say."

"How about thank you? Here let's put it on." She took it out of the box and strapped it onto his right wrist after removing his ancient *Timex*. "Doesn't this look a lot better?" She deposited the *Timex* into the trashcan, then raised her head and sniffed the air. "What's cooking?"

"Steaks. Come, they're just about done." He pulled her into the kitchen.

"Wait. I talked to Dad today. He wanted to be the one to tell you, but I badgered him, and he finally caved." She faced him and grabbed his arms. "Dad loves your homeless story, and he said the photos are the icing on the cake. Don't be surprised if this will make the front page tomorrow."

"You mean it?"

She nodded emphatically.

"Wow!" His arms went around her in a squeeze.

"Let me go. I'm famished and need to eat."

They sat on the balcony sipping brandy as the sun's red, fiery ball began its slow descent. Ribbons of many shades of pink and red stretched across the horizon.

"It's going to be a beautiful day tomorrow," Kyle mused, his thoughts drifting back to Graceville and the late walks he used to take along the beach when the ocean mirrored a sunset such as this. *One of these days I'll have to take Amy there.*

"Amy," he said turning to face her. Her head was resting on her chin, and a faint snore escaped her lips, the brandy snifter dangerous tipping toward her skirt. He quickly rescued the crimson liquid and looked at her. Shaking his head, he rose, picked her up carefully, and tiptoed inside. He placed her on the bed, and took her shoes off. She stirred slightly, and he stepped back, but she turned to her side.

"Pleasant dreams, my love," he whispered and covered her with the sheet. After cleaning up the kitchen, he went into the living room and relaxed on the sofa. Sleep claimed him shortly.

The phone shrilled, intruding rudely into Kyle's slumber. He answered.

"Kyle, Richard Sloan here."

"Yes, Sir," Kyle checked his new watch. 7:00 A.M.

"You may want to pick up a copy of the Journal." Richard chuckled and hung up.

Kyle dashed out of the apartment in his bare feet. He pushed the elevator button impatiently and then decided to take the stairs. He arrived breathlessly in the lobby and waved to Russell, the doorman, as he ran by him. Russell grinned and raised his hand. Kyle stopped at the news box on the corner, deposited the money, and pulled out the morning copy of *The Portland Journal.* The front page jumped at him with such intensity, his eyes welled. "Eddie, Portrait of a Homeless Man," he read. The paper had printed his article word for word accompanied by a picture of Eddie and two other photos of the area Eddie called home. Kyle leaped into the air, his arms raising the paper above his head. Passersby stared and shook their heads as they hurried past him. Kyle dropped more money into the box, retrieved three more copies, clutched them beneath his arm, and jogged back to Amy's apartment.

Russell spotted him and tipped his hat. "You okay this morning?"

"Okay? I'm terrific. Look," Kyle said and shoved the front page in front of Russell's alarming eyes. "I wrote this. These are my photos."

Recognition spread across Russell's face. "You're the photographer that's staying with Miss Amy."

It briefly occurred to Kyle that this was none of Russell's business, but he was too happy this morning to challenge the doorman's comment.

"I'll have to go buy a copy," he heard Russell say as he run up the steps two at a time.

Later that morning, Kyle stopped at the post office. *This will be a complete surprise, Mom, although I'm dying to tell you in person.* He paid the postage for mailing the large envelope. *I'm saving the best for last, the show. Wait until you hear about that.* He left the building whistling. Life had never been better. For the first time, he was in love, and his career was moving forward quickly. He decided to walk home. When he passed a homeless man dozing on the sidewalk, he stuck a five-dollar bill into his hand.

He took a detour and stopped at Quentin's studio.

"Hey, I saw your article. Front page, no less. You've arrived, Kyle," Quentin greeted him cheerfully.

Kyle blushed.

"Don't let your initial success go to your head. Never stop working hard. Which reminds me," he shuffled some papers on his desk and pulled out a sheet. "Here." He handed it to Kyle.

Images in Black and White by Kyle Weldon The bold, black font jumped out at Kyle, and he gasped. One of the photos he took at the Viet Nam protest appeared in the background. It featured the dates and times of the exhibit and ended with *Sponsored by Quentin's Art Studio.*

Kyle was stunned. His eyes scanned the paper repeatedly.

"Well, what do you think?" Quentin grinned broadly.

"Quentin, this looks awesome." He blinked and said, "I don't know what to say, except I'm thrilled, and in your debt. I'll never be able to thank...."

"No need to thank me," Quentin interjected. "This is going to be a profitable venture for both of us." He patted Kyle on the shoulder. "Don't ever forget what a marvelous talent you have, the pleasure you bring to people with your work. That's what this is all about." His eyes fell on the flyer. "So, you think it's all right? No need to change anything?"

"It's perfect."

"Well, I'll go ahead and have it printed. I'm also having several posters made to be placed in conspicuous places," Quentin said and laughed.

During the following weeks, the paper kept Kyle busy with what he considered mundane assignments, but he worked hard and people began recognizing him and responding to his work. A few letters to the editor arrived, praising his photographic skills.

One day he received a call from the South Dakota Office of Tourism. They wanted him to take photos for a promotional publication.

"We don't want ordinary pictures. We want you to capture the unique beauty of our state as it is seldom presented. Do you know what I'm saying?" Molly Grafton said.

"I think so."

"I have seen your work and you come highly recommended by Richard Sloan, a personal friend."

"I see," said Kyle.

"Not quite. Your work must excel our expectations. There are other photographers vying for this assignment. You must fly out here at your expense. If your work is chosen, we'll compensate you for your travelling expenses. How does that sound to you?"

"G...Great..." he caught himself. This is not the time to stutter. "I'm ready whenever you say." He straightened up, held his head high, and continued, "I will give you my best, and I guarantee you'll not be disappointed."

Molly smiled at the other end of the line. *Well, is he full of it or not? On the other hand, I like a person who has self-confidence. Besides, Richard Sloan rarely steers me wrong.* "Okay," she said, "when can you leave?"

"I'll book a flight for tomorrow." He took down her information and hung up. He dashed outside the apartment and hammered the elevator button, but gave up on waiting and took the stairs. He flew by Russell who watched with open mouth. Kyle stuck the key into Amy's mailbox. It was empty. He checked his watch, slammed the little door shut, and hurried back upstairs. Russell's eyes followed him and he grinned.

Inside the apartment, Kyle paced the floor. His credit card balance was creeping up to dangerous levels. Hopefully his paycheck would arrive today. He sighed, pulled out his phone, and booked a flight.

"Anybody home?"

"In here," Kyle answered. Amy appeared in the doorway carrying the mail.

"Oh, good." He hurried toward her and reached for the letters, but she turned, dashed into the living room and stopped. Hiding the mail behind her, she said, "First things first."

He took her into his arms and kissed her hard. The letters tumbled to the floor as she pulled him over to the couch and they made love.

Afterwards she whispered into his ear, "You may look at the mail now."

He jumped up, walked on top of their clothes strewn all over the floor, and picked up the letters. He searched through them and then exclaimed, "Here it is. Finally."

She sat up and slipped into his shirt. "Now you're rich," she said.

"Not quite, but it helps" He walked into the bedroom, and she followed.

"Going somewhere?" She pointed at the open suitcase.

He spun around. "Yes. I was offered an assignment in South Dakota. I'm leaving tomorrow."

"You're going to leave me all alone?" she mocked.

"It'll only be for a few days. This is a great opportunity for me."

She didn't answer.

"Amy?"

She remained quiet, her beautiful mouth drawn into a pout.

He took her into his arms. "I'll miss you terribly," he said. "I'll be back as soon as I can." He drew back and studied her face. A wisp of hair obscured her left eye, and he gently pushed it aside.

"I understand, and I'm happy for you. You go out there and give it your all, but in the meantime I need a bit attention from you." She kicked the suitcase off the bed and pulled him down. Her hands tore at the buttons of his shirt that she was wearing, and it occurred to him her sexual appetite was boundless, but his love for her swept him away.

CHAPTER 13

———

KYLE LOADED HIS LUGGAGE INSIDE the rental car and climbed into the driver's seat. He checked the highway and wove into the heavy airport traffic. Arriving at the hotel in Hill City, he checked in. Seated on the end of one of the double beds, he pulled out his phone and entered the numbers.

"Molly Grafton's office," a friendly voice answered.

"May I speak with Ms. Grafton, please? Kyle Weldon calling."

"Just a minute, please."

Molly's voice came through the line directly. "Kyle, are you settled in?"

"Yes, and I'm ready to go to work."

"Are you familiar with our state?"

"Now I am. I bought a couple of books and read up on it on the plane."

"Good. Let me stress, I don't want photos of Mt. Rushmore or Crazy Horse monuments, well, maybe one or two, but what I want from you is to capture the unusual, the wild and unrestrained beauty of our state. Get my drift?"

"Yes, I do. Give me a couple of days, and I'll be back in touch with you."

"Perfect." Molly hung up. *I think I like this guy. Let's see what he's going to bring me.*

Hill City was a small, picturesque town. He had planned to stay in Rapid City, but the clerk at the car rental persuaded him to change his plans. He left the hotel, strolled down Main Street, and stopped at the Alpine Inn for dinner. After he finished the filet mignon, followed by a homemade apple pie, he wiped his mouth and leaned back in his chair. Next to his Mom's cooking, this meal was one of the best he had in a long time. He paid and stepped out onto the porch. People relaxed in comfortable rocking chairs, watching the tourists passing by.

"Evenin'." An elderly man coming up the porch steps, pointed to Kyle's camera, and added, "Beautiful sunset."

Kyle nodded, approached the end of the porch and took several shots. The next day he drove the Peter Norbeck Scenic Byway which included the Needles Highway. The hairpin turns wound their way through narrow tunnels flanked by a maze of granite formations reminiscent of needles, organ pipes, and spires. He stopped often. The road continued to Custer State Park where large herds of bison grazed in the afternoon sun. He lost all track of time. He was one with the camera and its targets. On the way back, he stopped at Mount Rushmore, and then drove the short distance to the incomplete Crazy Horse Monument. He walked through the large hall featuring the Lakota Indians selling their wares, and stopped at a table where an old Indian woman sat embroidering a blouse. She looked up at him and smiled. Her wrinkled face resembled an old parchment map, but her eyes were bright and clear. She grabbed a white gauze shirt embroidered with wild flowers and held it up. "For your wife?" she said.

Kyle smiled and shook his head. "I'm not married."

"Ah," she said. "Girlfriend maybe?"

He nodded and took the shirt from her. "Did you make this?"

"Yes," she said.

"I'll take it." It looked like the right size for Amy. He pulled out his wallet, and paid her, then lifted his camera, and pointed it at the sculpture of Crazy Horse displayed just outside the large hall. Placed strategically against the background of the unfinished monument, its white marble glistened in the sun. The Indians owned the mountain which eventually would be turned into the mighty warrior sitting on his stallion and pointing angrily in the distance, where the land of the Lakota used to stretch for many miles.

The old Indian woman wrapped the blouse in tissue.

"Thanks," he said and turned to the woman. "May I take your picture?"

She smiled shyly and stood very straight looking at him.

"No," he said, "here, next to the sculpture."

"Okay," she nodded and posed proudly next to the pure white marble image of the great warrior. Kyle took several shots, and when she returned to her table, he took some more.

When he got back to the hotel, he stretched out on the bed. His mind reviewed all he had seen today and he knew he unequivocally had fallen in love with South Dakota.

Early the next morning, he drove to the Badlands National Park. He parked the car and walked with his camera ready. The peaks, gullies, buttes, and wide prairies of the badlands fascinated him. The whole region seemed like a part of another world. Although barren and dry, wildlife abounded in the Badlands. Kyle saw butterflies, turtles, bluebirds, and a prairie dog. The latter disappeared quickly into his den before Kyle could get a shot, so he waited patiently in the hot sun. He was not going to be disappointed because half an hour later the prairie dog re-appeared and Kyle snapped his picture.

From the badlands, he drove to Deadwood where Wild Bill Hickok and Calamity Jane used to roam. He visited their graves at Mt. Moriah Cemetery. An empty bottle of whiskey sat next to the gravestone of Wild Bill.

His final stop was the Adams House. Kyle had always been interested in architecture and had seen pictures of the mansion before. Built by Harris and Anna Franklin in the early 1890s, it boasted central heating, hot and cold running water and electric lights. Servants were summoned by electric bells, and the home's occupants communicated by telephone—the ideal of a modern American house in any urban center at the time. Golden oak woodwork surrounded the rooms, many of which featured pocket doors. Hearths of onyx and tiles in decorative bas relief, stunning light fixtures, and elaborate bathroom appointments highlighted the rooms. Kyle passed through the house experiencing a return to the cultural living of the American west following one of the country's last great gold rushes.

He returned to his car and drove to Rapid City where he stopped at a CVS and had his photos printed at the photo machine. Then grabbed a bite to eat and called Amy. She didn't answer.

When he arrived at the hotel, he phoned her again. No answer. *I wonder where she is.* He missed her. He spread out the photos on the bed and studied them.

The next morning, he dropped all the photos off at Molly's office. He was pleased and found it difficult to eliminate any. He wrote a note: *Molly, I'm giving you all the photos I took. Thank you for offering me this opportunity. I can't express how much I enjoyed your beautiful state. Thanks so much. Kyle.*

He flagged down a taxi that took him to the airport.

CHAPTER 14

———◆———

THE LOW DRONING OF THE plane's engine lulled Kyle to sleep, and as soon as he closed his eyes, Amy's face appeared. He had tried to call her again from the airport before he boarded the plane. Still no answer.

It was the first time he was in love, and his emotions wreaked havoc with his intellect. Doubts assailed him constantly. Amy was a sophisticated, worldly woman. What would she want with a backwoods neophyte from Graceville? He shifted his six- foot frame in the cramped space and tried to stretch his legs. He ran his hand through his hair as his thoughts drifted back to Amy. *Where could she be?* Surely she had a life before she met him, but now that they were together, there would be no one but him, right? No, he mustn't think like that. He picked up an airline magazine and leafed through it. Amy's face appeared on every page, and he forced his eyes shut. He was certain he loved her. Maybe they would get married, have a family, not just yet, but in time. His career was just getting off the ground. Pictures of South Dakota streamed in front of his eyes, and Kyle's head rolled to the side, and the magazine slipped to the floor.

When he arrived at the apartment, the place was a mess; dirty glasses and plates with leftover bruschetta and shrimp scampi littered the living room. The stale air assaulted his nostrils, and he opened the kitchen window. Empty champagne bottles cluttered the counter. He walked into the bedroom. Amy's clothes covered the floor. She lay on her stomach, sound asleep. He strode across the room, bent down and kissed her on the neck. She moaned and pushed him away.

"What happened here? Did you have a party?" he said.

She opened her eyes slowly and stared at him, uncomprehending. "Oh, it's you," she muttered and pushed him away. "Let me sleep. I'm exhausted."

"I guess so. It must have been quite a bash."

She shot up. Her beautiful eyes filled with anger. "So what! This is my place. I can do whatever I want. It's none of your business. We're not married." Her head dropped back onto the pillows and she pulled the sheet over it.

Stunned, Kyle stood by the bed watching her. She was already asleep. He turned and left the bedroom and began cleaning up the mess. He made coffee and read the newspaper he had picked up at the airport.

An hour later, she appeared in the kitchen door way wearing a terry cloth robe. "Hi." She rubbed her head. "I feel awful. I need some coffee." He didn't answer, so she poured herself a cup and stood sipping it while watching him.

He ignored her, although his heart was pounding. He was ready to pull her into his arms and forgive and forget whatever happened. He ached to kiss her and hold her and never let her go.

"What's your problem? Aren't you glad to see me? I'm happy you're back." She walked over to him and placed her hand on his forearm. Her touch was more than he could handle, and he rose and pulled her to him.

"Hey, wait a minute," she pushed back a little. Her hands touched his cheeks, they were wet. "Tears?" she said and hugged him tight. "Sweetheart, I'm not worth any tears, believe me. If you were smart, you would run as fast as you could and not look back."

"Run?" he said. "I want to marry you. I love you."

Her arms dropped, and she threw her head back and laughed hysterically. "Love? Now that's a powerful word, one that's not in my vocabulary." She gestured for him to sit down and took a chair opposite him. "Look, let's get something straight right now. We're enjoying each other, having a good time, but love is out of the question. I need my freedom.

You're just a kid. What can you offer me? I'm going to get bored with you, if I'm not already...."

"That's not what I want," he interrupted. "I told you I love you. I want marriage, a family, grow old together. Obviously I was wrong to think we could have that." He stared at her incredulously, his breath labored, heavy, and quick.

She kept talking. "Let's just have fun. You do your thing, and I'll do mine."

He rose sharply and the chair crashed to the floor. His fist pounded the table. "Shut up!" he yelled.

He walked into the bedroom, gathered his few things, and stuffed them into his suitcase. His eyes fell on the tissue package holding the blouse he bought for her from the Indian woman. He threw it onto the bed. On the way out, he grabbed his mail from the dresser and without looking at her, he left the apartment.

She stared after him stunned. She had him figured all wrong. He surprised her by his actions, and deep down she mustered some respect she hadn't felt for him before. *Oh well, I was getting bored with him. Good riddance.* She rose and walked into the bedroom when she saw the white package. She tore it open, and discovered the beautifully embroidered blouse. She laughed out loud. *Did he really think I would wear this piece of garbage?* She flung it into the corner and headed for the shower.

Kyle walked past Russell, the doorman, who stared at Kyle's luggage. Kyle navigated the revolving door and stepped outside. He stopped and took a deep breath. He wanted to crawl into a corner and lick his wounds or, better yet, get stone drunk. First things first. He needed a place to stay. He turned right and walked to the fast food restaurant at the corner where he bought a newspaper on his way inside. After he paid for coffee and a bacon and egg sandwich, he took a seat and studied classifieds. He found several furnished apartments listed that would serve his purpose. One of them was located only five blocks away. He finished his food and left.

He rang the doorbell. An elderly gentleman opened the door. "Yes?"

"I'm interested in the apartment," Kyle said pointing to the newspaper under his arm. The man scrutinized Kyle, and then looked at the luggage. He raised his head and his eyes locked with Kyle's.

"Come in," he finally said, and Kyle entered a small foyer. The man pointed to the stairway and handed him a key. "It's on the fourth floor. Used to be the attic, so watch your head."

Kyle hesitated.

"Well, go ahead," the man said. "I only venture up there when it's absolutely necessary. I'll be waiting here."

Kyle climbed the stairway. Once he passed the third floor the steps narrowed considerably, and he inched himself up sideways. He arrived at the door and unlocked it. He entered a tiny hallway that led to a small kitchen with a bathroom to the right and a living room to the left. A battered sofa and chair and a small bookcase filled the tiny room. The ceilings were slanted, so he stayed within the center of the room to avoid bumping his head. *This will take some getting used to.* Crossing the living room, he checked out the bedroom. There was a double bed with a night table and a small dresser. Facing south, he stepped into a small circular addition to the room surrounded by windows. He walked inside and held his breath. The view was fabulous. The only furniture here consisted of a small desk and a painted arm chair. He stood for a long time studying the Portland landscape below. The place was perfect, but could he afford it? He turned and left the apartment bumping his head on the living room ceiling on his way out. He had ventured too far to the left. He rubbed his head and smiled. *I'll get used to it.*

He descended the stairs and joined the man who stood patiently.

"Well, what do you think? By the way, my name is William McDougal." He stretched out his hand.

"Kyle Weldon," Kyle said and shook McDougal's hand. "I like the place. It's perfect for me. How much is it?"

"Well," William's eyes swept over Kyle and his luggage, "how about..." he paused and scratched his head. "How about $450 a month, including utilities?"

"Great. I'll pay you $50 now and the rest this afternoon after I've been to the bank." He pointed to an envelope he was certain contained a check.

"Okay, you got yourself a place."

"Thanks. I'll see you this afternoon." Kyle picked up his luggage and headed upstairs. He dropped the two bags onto the bedroom floor and fell on the bed. Within minutes, he was fast asleep.

He kept busy during the following weeks. Assignments trickled in slowly, just enough to help him meet his expenses. The nights were the worst. He found himself hanging around Amy's apartment hoping to catch a glimpse of her. His stops at the little bar around the corner became more frequent.

The date of the show approached. All the invitations had been sent out. Quentin advised Kyle to buy a decent suit. This would not be a casual event.

"Hi, Mom."

"Kyle, it's great to hear your voice. How are you?"

"Fine, I guess. Well not really. I'm nervous as heck and can't wait to see you and Luke. I need you here with me."

"We're leaving early in the morning. Did you make reservations for us?"

"Yes. The hotel is close to the studio." He gave her the specifics. "Sorry I can't put you up at my apartment. It's just too small."

"Don't worry, dear. We understand. Can't wait to see it though." Joan tried to picture Kyle making beds, doing laundry, dusting and so forth. The thought made her smile. "See you tomorrow."

She hung up and turned away, when the phone rang again. "Did you forget something, Kyle?"

"Mrs. Weldon, it's Lisa."

"Hi, Lisa. I was just talking to Kyle. We're leaving for Portland tomorrow."

"Mrs. Weldon, I was wondering," she fell silent and fidgeted with the silver necklace she wore. "Well, I wanted to know if I could join you?" she finally said.

Joan carefully chose her words. "I don't think it's a good idea, Lisa. There will be other times. Besides, Kyle has promised to come home over the holidays. You can see him then."

"I guess you're right." Lisa swallowed hard and continued. "I miss him so much, Mrs. Weldon. If he would let me spend time with him, I could convince him..."

"Lisa, it's not a good idea right now," Joan interrupted.

"I guess you're right. Please give him my best wishes and tell him I'm so proud of him."

"I will. Bye, Lisa."

"Hi Mom," Luke came into the kitchen and dropped his books onto the table. "What's up?"

"Lisa just called."

"She did?" He came closer. "What'd she want?"

"She wants to go to Portland with us to attend Kyle's show. I told her it's not a good idea."

"I think it's an excellent idea, although, I don't know why she wants to waste her time on Kyle. He's not interested. Never was." He opened the refrigerator and reached for the milk jug. "She needs to realize there are so many other fish in the sea." He glanced furtively at his mother.

Joan stood with her arms folded, trying to muster her thoughts. Deep down, she agreed with Luke, although Lisa was the perfect girl for Kyle. But now there seemed to be another woman in the picture, one Kyle had never mentioned. *Or maybe that's a thing of the past, since he no longer lives with her. He's got his own place now. I wonder what she's like. I don't think I would like her.* Joan dropped her arms and left the kitchen.

Luke put down his glass and the line of his mouth tightened. *One of these days, you'll know who is the right guy for you, Lisa. I'll make sure of it, and it won't be Kyle.*

CHAPTER 15

———————

THE MORNING OF THE EXHIBIT Kyle woke up at dawn. He jumped out of bed careful to dodge the ceiling. His new suit hung on a hook over the bedroom door. His hand brushed across the charcoal sharkskin. It felt cool and luxurious. The blue striped tie he picked accentuated the darker color of the suit. He slipped into a shirt and khakis and left for the deli around the corner for coffee and a bagel. When he returned, he lounged on the couch hoping the coffee would calm the butterflies in his stomach. He checked his watch: 8.00 AM. After he emptied his coffee cup, he grabbed his camera and headed out the door. He navigated the stairs quietly and stepped outside. A brisk breeze welcomed him, and he squinted at the sun. The clear blue sky assured a good day, and he was relieved. It was a good sign, yet doubts began to torture his mind. What if no one showed up?

When Kyle mentioned his concern about lack of attendance to Quentin, he had laughed and said, "Your apprehensions are normal, but not warranted. Try to dismiss them. Once you get a few shows under your belt, you'll be able to control your nerves."

Kyle approached the small park with the children's play area and sat on the bench. Amy was never far from his mind. The anguish of missing her cut like a knife. He had never experienced this kind of agony. Many times he opened his phone to call her, but flipped it shut. Her rejection of his marriage proposal had crushed him. He had found some solace in liquor to the point where lately he had gotten drunk more often than he would like to admit. Intellectually, he knew liquor wasn't the answer, but it gave him comfort.

Two screaming birds roused him from his thoughts. They tugged on a dried up worm until it split in half. Kyle raised his camera. The flash scared the birds, and they took off, leaving their breakfast behind.

I need a drink. He jumped up and jogged home. He dashed up the stairs, two at a time, unlocked the apartment door, and slammed it behind him. The whiskey bottle sitting on the kitchen counter was almost empty. He raised it to his mouth and drank.

Kyle grew aware of a distant ringing, and lifted his head. He groaned and pulled out his phone.

"Kyle, we're waiting for you. Did you forget?"

"Mom." His eyes fell on his watch. He was supposed to meet Joan and Luke for brunch at two o'clock. He swallowed a silent curse. "I fell asleep. I'm sorry. I'll be there in fifteen minutes."

"That's fine. We'll be in the lobby. See you soon."

"Okay." He disconnected and ran into the bathroom. He blinked as he looked at his face. He resembled one of the homeless people he had been writing about, with his hair mussed, bloodshot eyes, and stubble on his chin. *Good God, I'm a mess. I've got to pull myself together. I don't want my family to know about Amy, and how stupid I've been.*

"Here's the address, Mom." Kyle jotted it down on a piece of paper. "Take a cab and be there at six o'clock sharp." He gave her a hug, bestowed a friendly slap on Luke's back, and left the hotel restaurant. Lunch had been non-eventful. They made mostly small talk. Kyle was sure his Mom picked up on his mood, although he tried very hard to be cheerful and upbeat, he knew he hadn't been able to fool her.

Back at his apartment, he changed into his new suit. Ready to go, he was about to open the door when he saw his camera sitting on the table. Should he take it? He rarely went without it. He hesitated for a moment, and then decided against taking it. He skipped down the steps. William met him at the front door. "Wow, look at you." The warmth of his smile echoed in his voice. He had grown to like Kyle who was a respectful and responsible tenant.

"I'm heading for the studio," Kyle said a little breathless. "Man, am I anxious!"

"I'll be sure to drop by," William reached out and straightened Kyle's tie, "after I get cleaned up a bit for this occasion."

"See you then," Kyle said as he ran out the door.

He arrived at Quentin's studio twenty minutes later. A large poster announcing the event rested on a decorative easel next to the entrance door. Kyle looked at his picture beneath the headline and his heart began to flutter. *This is real. I still can't believe it.*

"You'd better believe it." Quentin joined him carrying a bunch of balloons.

Kyle chuckled. "You read my mind."

"At this point, it isn't difficult to do. This is a big opportunity for you, and you deserve it."

"I don't know how I can ever thank you…"

"I'm glad to be of help," Quentin interrupted. "Remember, this is just the beginning. You have the talent, and as long as you're willing to work hard, you'll go far. I'm rarely wrong about these things. Come in." He patted Kyle on the back and they went inside the studio. "How about some coffee?" Quentin said. Kyle had walked away studying the framed photos lining both sides of the wall.

Kyle smiled when he saw the picture of his neighbor Ernie and his dog frolicking on the beach in Graceville. He clearly remembered the morning he took this photo. He continued walking. Bitter-sweet tears rose as his eyes roamed the black and white prints spanning much of his youth. *I did this. This is my work, and it looks pretty damn good.* He smiled inwardly and began to relax. His step became more upbeat, his back straightened, and his chin rose.

"Quite impressive, isn't it?" Quentin had joined him. "Now, remember, you must mingle. Talk to people. Make them feel welcome and, above all, be proud of your work and show it."

"Yes, sir." Kyle said. The door opened. Joan and Luke had arrived. Kyle hurried toward them.

"Kyle, I'm so proud of you." Joan embraced him, as she struggled to hide the tears in her eyes. Reluctantly, she let go and looked around. Luke was already strolling down the show room floor examining the photos on the wall.

"Look at these beautiful pictures. Our house..." Joan pointed to a framed photo. "I remember when you shot this one. You were only ten years old."

Kyle watched her as she kept on walking. Many of the photos displayed represented parts of their lives. So many memories, preserved forever on paper.

Joan stepped closer to the wall, her hand raised to her face and tears rolling down her cheeks. He knew she was looking at the photo of his dad fixing the rudder on the sailboat. Gregg Weldon never knew he was being photographed, and he never saw the photo. He died three days later.

Hushed voices filled the room. The gallery was filling up with people. Quentin nudged him as he passed by him, whispering, "Mingle! Remember, mingle!"

Kyle checked his watch. It was almost closing time, yet people still lingered. Many empty spaces on the walls stared at Kyle. People actually liked his photographs enough to purchase them. The thought filled him with pride and pleasure. At this moment, all he wanted was to produce even better photography. Joan and Luke had left about an hour before. He planned to catch up with them after the show. It occurred to him he only thought of Amy when her dad showed up. After scrutinizing the collection, Richard Sloan approached Kyle.

"Congratulations, Kyle. This is impressive." He shook Kyle's hand. "We're going to cover this event in the paper. After all, you're part of the staff, and we like to show you off." He pointed to a young man carrying notepad and camera "Steven here will interview you and, with your permission, take some photos."

"Of course, thank you, Mr. Sloan. I *am* very grateful. You made it all happen when you gave me a chance."

"Well, it was Amy who set everything in motion..." he paused and studied Kyle's face which had tightened and turned stony. "I'm sorry, son, about the way things worked out between you two. She is my daughter, and I love her, but it's painful to see how she wastes her life and talent. Frankly, I'm glad it's over between you two. Her relationships with men never last long, and the breakup was inevitable from the beginning."

"Don't worry about me; I'll be fine."

Five minutes to eight and still a few people lingered. Kyle stood near the front door talking with Quentin when it opened, and Amy entered the gallery accompanied by a young man wearing a tuxedo. She looked stunning in a grey sequined dress that hugged her slender body and accentuated her curves.

"Hello, Kyle," she said and brushed his cheek with a kiss. She didn't bother to introduce her friend, and before Kyle could say a word, she floated past him. Kyle's blue eyes turned stony, and he struggled to keep his breathing normal.

Quentin laid a restraining hand on his shoulder, and whispered into his ear, "Careful, my boy. She's a stick of dynamite, and you don't want to play into her hands. Keep your cool. Ignore her." He emphasized the last two words. "Consider this: we sold 65 photographs. Look at the walls, they're almost empty."

Amy's shrill laughter resonated through the gallery. Kyle could tell she had been drinking. "Mr. Weldon," she shouted and pointed to a photo of a lonely seagull foraging on the beach.

Kyle hesitated when Quentin gave him a push. "Remember, keep calm," he hissed.

Kyle approached Amy. She threw her purse into the hands of her escort and stepped forward to remove the painting-sized framed photo from the wall. "Now doesn't that remind me of someone," she sneered and looked straight into his eyes. "A lonely seagull...."

"Ma'am, since you took the picture off the wall, you have to purchase it." Kyle said coolly.

"Oh, do I now?" She threw her head back and barked an ugly laugh. "Well, let me tell you something, you child, you paragon of naiveté." She stopped and turned to him, "I've just made a decision. I'll buy all of them. The whole caboodle. What do you have to say about that?"

"They're not for sale…"

"Oh, but they are." Quentin came running. "We deliver. Where would you like me to send them?"

Amy reached for her purse and dug inside. She presented Quentin with her business card. She searched again, came up with a credit card and handed it to him. Triumphantly, she looked over her shoulder, but Kyle had left the gallery.

CHAPTER 16

———◆———

THE CUSTOMERS FILED OUT OF the bar, except for one. Kyle sat slumped at the counter signaling for another drink. The bar-tender, weary and tired, approached him. "Look, buddy, don't you think you've had enough? Besides we're closing. Why don't you go home and sleep it off?"

Kyle raised his head. His eyes were bloodshot, his hair disheveled. Liquor had splattered across his loosened tie and covered it with ugly stains. His lids drooped as he tried to focus.

The bartender shook his head. "Whoever she is, she ain't worth it, trust me. For the last time, we're closed." He took off his apron and threw it behind the counter.

Kyle dragged himself off the barstool. He stopped to secure his balance and shuffled across the room. At the door, he said over his shoulder. "Thanks for nothing, chum." He searched for an expletive but remained tongue-tied. Though he tried to slam the door, the air piston defied him.

His search for a taxi proved futile. He pulled his jacket together with one hand, raised his collar, and dragging his feet, headed for home.

When he arrived at the house, he crept up the stairs. He reached his door and searched in vain for the key. Finally, he gave up, dropped to the floor, and passed out.

"Kyle, wake-up." Someone shook him, and he opened his eyes to a squint. William stood over him. "What happened? Did you spend the night out here?" Without waiting for an answer he said, "Your mom has been trying to reach you. She's worried about you."

Kyle blinked without comprehension as William unlocked the door, pulled him up with two strong arms, and guided him inside the apartment. "Now you wait here. I'll be right back." He patted Kyle on the arm and labored downstairs.

A heart wrenching sob shook Kyle's body, and he covered his face. When William returned Kyle had lowered his head and refused to look at him.

"Here, drink this." William handed him a steaming cup of coffee. "You'll feel much better after this."

With his head turned, Kyle whispered, "I'm sorry."

"There's no need." William studied Kyle quietly. "Do you think you're the first guy who has been ditched by a dame?"

"How do you know...?"

"I recognize the symptoms. I've been there. If you're smart, you'll learn from this experience." William gave Kyle an encouraging smile. "Call your mom," he said and left the apartment.

Joan rushed to answer the phone. "Hello..." she hesitated. She had not slept all night. She kept waiting for the phone to ring to deliver any news about Kyle. Only Quentin called to assure her Kyle was alright.

"He's got good common sense, with one exception," Quentin said, and then he told her about the disastrous relationship Kyle had with Amy. Joan's heart ached for Kyle.

Luke took a totally different view. "At least, he had fun while it lasted," he had said with a shrug.

"Mom," Kyle began with a shaky voice. "Look, Mom, I'm sorry about last night. I know I was rude..."

"Kyle," she gently interrupted. "I'm so happy to hear from you. Are you okay?"

Kyle shivered. He moved his shoulders beneath the crumbled shirt. His skin felt clammy and dirty. A long shower would help. Pictures of Amy assailed his mind. It was worse when he shut his eyes. He must get her out of his thoughts. An unconscious sob escaped aloud.

"Kyle, can you hear me?"

His head jerked back. "Yes, Mom," he said. "Look, I'm going to get cleaned up, and then I'll be over. What time are you guys leaving?"

"Right after breakfast. I have to report for work this afternoon."

Kyle released an exasperated sigh. "Mr. Rappel is a slave driver. Don't let him push you around…"

"He isn't anything like that. I'm grateful he's given me this job." She was a little angry. Lack of sleep didn't help her disposition. Her son would never know what she went through last night. She was glad he was okay, but he was the last person who should hand out advice.

"See you in a little while, Mom. Love you." Kyle hung up.

"Morning," Kyle stuck his head through the door of Quentin's studio. "Are you still speaking to me?"

Quentin perused a folder he held in his hands. He looked up and smiled. "Come let me show you what a success you were yesterday. We sold every one of your photos."

Kyle frowned. "Yes, I know. Amy…"

"No, it wasn't just Amy. By the time she arrived we had sold 85% of the displayed pieces. This show was a tremendous success. Sure, Amy clinched it by buying the remaining photos, but we didn't need her purchases to come out way ahead. I'll total everything this morning, and I'll cut you a check. Give me a couple of hours." He happily slapped Kyle's shoulder and walked away—and then suddenly turned. "Oh, I almost forgot. A guy named Eddie stopped by looking for you. He wants to talk to you. He said you know where to find him."

"Thanks. See you later." Kyle said and left. Outside he was debating whether to take a cab or walk the few miles to the Portland Café, when a taxi slowed down in front of him. Kyle signaled and climbed into the back seat. They sped to the Portland Café.

Kyle paid the driver and pushed through the door. Eddie sat at the counter talking to Neill. He rose and gave him a wide grin.

"Hey, here comes the celebrity." He shook Kyle's hand heartily and dragged him over to a table. "Lunch is on me."

Kyle threw up his hands, "No, I can't let you do that..."

"But you must," Eddie said with mocking solemnity. "I'm employed. Thanks to you, I've got a job."

"That's great, Eddie. What do you do?" Kyle gestured to Neill to give him a beer.

"I'm the official janitor at the Seeing Eye, an optical place, on Weatherby Road. They contacted me after they read your article in the Journal. I wanted to come to your show yesterday, but I had to work. Thanks to you, I'm getting back my self-respect. It feels good to work again, get a paycheck, and be able to take care of myself without depending on handouts. Look," he drew his lips back into a huge, toothless smile. "I'm getting dentures. The secretary put me in touch with a dentist who does charity work. How about that?"

"Excellent." Kyle said.

Neill approached. Eddie ordered coffee and a burger.

"Give me a beer," Kyle said. Neill waited.

"That's all."

Neill stepped away, shaking his head in disapproval. He returned almost immediately with their drinks. Kyle lifted the bottle and emptied it halfway. "Might as well get me another one, Neill."

Eddie studied him quietly for a few moments and then casually said, "Isn't it a little early for that?"

Kyle put down the bottle of beer. "For what?" he asked innocently.

"You know exactly what I mean..."

"Look, I had a very successful show yesterday, and I probably will make quite a bit of money. Is it wrong to celebrate a little?"

"I guess not," Eddie said doubtfully. "Just as long as you don't overdo it." He swallowed his coffee.

Neill approached slamming the second bottle of beer on the table. "How about some food?"

"I'm not hungry, Neill." Kyle lifted the beer bottle to his mouth and said, "Bring me a chaser."

Neill snorted contemptuously and plodded away.

"Look, Kyle, how about a sandwich before you hit the hard stuff?" Eddie said.

Kyle leaned back in his chair. "What're talking about, Eddie? I need something stronger to get moving." He made a dismissing gesture. "You don't have a clue what I'm trying to deal with."

Neill approached the table and slammed down the shot glass. The dark, coppery liquid spilled around the edges creating a crooked halo. Kyle grabbed the glass and emptied it before Neill had a chance to leave. "Here," Kyle said, and shoved the glass toward Neill. "Give me another, only make it a double this time and forget about the beer. It doesn't do anything for me," he sniggered and turned to Eddie. "You were saying?"

"I haven't said it yet, but I'm gonna." Eddie pushed his coffee cup back. "I never thought I'd see the day..."

"What? To see me drunk?" Kyle laughed viciously. "But I'm not drunk yet." Kyle emptied the glass in front of him, and slammed it on the table. "Bring me the bottle," he called out to Neill.

"Hell, I've seen and heard enough." Eddie jumped up, reached inside his pocket and threw some money onto the table. He proceeded to walk away, but hesitated, and with his mouth close to Kyle's ear, he said, "You've been an inspiration to me. I owe you a lot, which is the only reason I'm not going to give you the crap you deserve. I don't know what happened, but you're a damn fool. You're heading for the abyss and don't know it. Believe me, I've been there. It ain't fun." He straightened up and added, "I'm your friend. Remember that."

Kyle did not answer. He just stared at the table in front of him, and then picked up the bottle and drank. He dropped his head and closed his eyes, and the vision of Amy floating into the studio last night filled him with despair. He brought his hands up to his head and squeezed as if he could dispel any thoughts of Amy, but her image remained, her beautiful face, her laughter, filled with derision. The pain was unbearable. He wiped his eyes and stared at his hands. The tears created a silky film in his palms. He sighed and rose. He tried to focus on Neill who had been watching him. Kyle gave him a crooked smile and raised his hands, "I know, I know, I'm a bad boy. Don't worry, I'm leaving."

"How about some coffee before you go?"

Keeping his head low, Kyle pushed the chair in. He could no longer face Neill, or anyone for that matter. He had to get away. "No thanks. I've got to go," he said and left.

Shaking his head, Neill stared after him. He liked Kyle a lot. He swore by first impressions, and Kyle had struck him as a young man who knew what he wanted out of life and go after it. Neill rubbed his chin; could he have been so wrong?

CHAPTER 17

———————

LUKE PULLED THE CAR INTO the driveway. The trip home had been quiet. He turned off the engine and said, "Don't you think Kyle acted weirdly? The show had been such a success. All those people, buying his photographs. He should've been happy, but he almost seemed sad."

Joan had decided not to tell Luke about the conversation she had with Quentin concerning Amy. It was up to Kyle to tell Luke if he chose to do so.

"Well, he's famous now," Luke said, and as an afterthought, he added, "I hope he doesn't get stuck up and thinks he's better than us...."

"Kyle would never do that," she interrupted, her voice raised.

"Okay. No need to get excited. I just meant..."

"I know what you meant. I'm certain Kyle won't let his success go to his head."

Luke rolled his eyes and got out of the car.

The car came to a slow stop in front of Lisa's house. Luke honked once. The front door opened and Lisa skipped down the steps. Luke exited the car and opened the passenger door for her.

"Thank you," she said and slid into the seat. When he called to ask her out for a soda she readily agreed. She knew he'd been to Portland to attend Kyle's event and she had a hundred questions she planned to spring on him. She knew Luke had a crush on her, and she fully intended to use him to get all the information she could about Kyle.

"How was your trip?" she began, even before Luke got back into the driver's seat.

"It was okay. I've been to Portland before and am not impressed."

"How is Kyle?" she said impatiently.

Luke stiffened. He did not want to talk about Kyle. He intended to concentrate on convincing her that he's the guy for her. "Kyle...you know, Kyle is Kyle."

"Yes, I know, but tell me, what's he doing? Is he coming back to Graceville soon?"

"No way. He hates small-town Graceville." He glanced at her sideways and added, "He's seeing some rich chick in Portland."

She didn't reply, but kept her lips pressed tightly together.

"You can kiss him goodbye. He is travelling in different circles. We won't see much of him." He paused.

Lisa held her breath. When he remained quiet, she demanded, "What woman? Who is she?"

"I don't know. He didn't say much. They're pretty tight. I imagine they'll get married." The lie rolled smoothly off his tongue.

"Married," she almost screamed the word. "Why, he can't know her well enough to get married." She fought to conquer her tears. "It takes time to know someone."

"I know what you mean," he interrupted. He weighed the words and against his better judgment he added, "I know, I've been in love with you since I was twelve. *Really*, in love. No other girl matters to me."

She ignored his confession. "When is he coming back to Graceville?" she demanded.

"Never. I told you he hates small-town Graceville."

She didn't answer. They had arrived at their destination, and he parked the car. Lisa sat still, her back straight and stiff. She wanted to go home, crawl into her bed, and cry. At this moment, she hated Luke and wanted to be far away from him.

Luke sat patiently throwing occasional surreptitious glances in her direction. He saw her pale face and trembling lips.

"Look," he said, "Why don't we forgot about Kyle and enjoy our lunch? I want to hear all about your job and the kids you're taking care of. What do you say?"

She nodded reluctantly and got out of the car. He hurried to her side, reached for her arm, and led her into the little café.

The next morning, he told his mom about his date with Lisa.

"She agreed to go out on a date with you?" Joan asked, amazed. "I know she hasn't seen anybody since Kyle left. She's hopelessly in love with him."

"I know, and I aim to change her mind, but after yesterday, I'm not so sure I can." He rose to fill his coffee cup.

Joan buttered her toast. "I tried to tell her it's hopeless. Kyle's not interested in her, but she refuses to accept it." She put down the knife. "How did it go?"

"What?"

"The date, how did it go?"

"Not very exciting. She wouldn't even let me hold her hand. We talked about her job at the daycare. There is one particular little boy she has taken a fancy to. He's an orphan, living in a foster home." Luke chuckled, "Get this, she wants to adopt him."

Joan raised her eyebrows. "Adopt?" She hesitated a minute and then added, "Why not? I think Lisa will make an excellent mother."

"But what about a father? She needs a husband and I could be that guy."

Joan almost choked on her coffee. She slammed down the cup. "You are in no position to be a father to anyone. You're still in college. It takes money…"

"I thought it all out. I could drop out, get a job, and go to night school. That's what Lisa's doing to get her master's degree. I would do anything for her if she would agree to be with me."

Joan leaned back in her chair. She must talk to Lisa. Luke's infatuation with her was all wrong.

"Well, gotta go." Luke rose and kissed her on the cheek. "Bye, Mom. See you tonight."

Joan nodded without saying a word and as soon as she heard the door slam, she wept. Sobbing she dropped her head onto her arms. The trilling of the phone roused her. She raised her head. It stopped. She dabbed at her swollen, red eyes and got up. She splashed cold water on her face and turned to lean against the counter when the phone rang again. This time she answered.

"Mrs. Weldon, it's Lisa."

Joan blinked. "I was just thinking about you."

"I know. Luke probably told you what happened. I'm sorry, Mrs. Weldon, I like Luke. He is a very nice boy, but I'll always love Kyle."

"Have you made that clear to Luke?"

"Of course. I also told him I can never go out on a date with him again." She paused. "I'm ashamed to admit I only went out with him to get news about Kyle."

"I see."

"I know it wasn't a nice thing to do. I swear it'll never happen again." Children's laughter rang in the back ground, and Lisa said, "I just wanted you to know. I've got to go. Bye, Mrs. Weldon."

"Bye, Lisa." Joan hung up. She smiled in relief and hurried up the steps to get ready for work.

CHAPTER 18

———◆———

KYLE WEARILY CLIMBED THE STAIRS to his apartment. His cell phone buzzed. He had a voice message.

"Kyle, I have a new assignment for you. Call me," Conley Brown's voice echoed in his ear. Kyle immediately dialed his number.

"Conley Brown."

"I got your message."

"Thanks for returning my call so promptly. I want you to do an article on the Marshall Point Lighthouse here in Maine. We need photos and the history, in detail."

Kyle caught his breath, and his heart began to beat faster. Since childhood his interest in lighthouses had only grown. Memories of visiting the steadfast beacons of hope along the Maine coast with his family rushed by like the turning of a kaleidoscope. He used to tell his dad, "If I can't be a photographer when I grow up, I want to be a lighthouse keeper."

"Why not be both?" his dad said with a smile. Now, most of the lights are automated, eliminating the need for a keeper.

"Kyle, did you hear me?"

"Yes. When do I leave?"

"Right away." Conley chuckled and then added, "All expenses are being paid by the paper. You've got a week. Does that give you enough time?"

"Absolutely."

"Save your receipts." Conley hung up.

Kyle dropped onto the sofa. Amy's face popped into his head, and he looked up and spotted the whiskey bottle. He shook his head and hurried into the bedroom, got his suitcase, and began to pack.

Huge Atlantic rollers hurled against the base of the lighthouse, receding reluctantly and leaving frothy peaks on the rocks. Screeching seagulls hovered overhead to catch an unfortunate sea creature trapped until the next surge came to its rescue.

Pacing the platform, Kyle raised his camera. The brisk gusts dampened his face as he scanned the sea. What a fantastic view. Scattered clouds appearing at the horizon threatened a change in the weather while shafts of the descending sun stabbed through the grey fluff.

Marshall Point Lighthouse rose, isolated at the southern tip of the St. George peninsula stretching into Muscongus Bay, off the rock-ribbed Maine coast. Kyle had arrived an hour ago. He focused his camera again and then changed his mind. He needed to find lodging and some food. He had not eaten since breakfast and spent his time taking many photos. Reluctantly, he decided it was time to leave. He bent his tall frame through the doorway into the small room housing the light and descended the stairs. He stepped onto the raised wooden walkway that connected the tower to the land where the keeper's house stood. Powerful waves slamming against the granite rocks washed his face with salty spray as the ubiquitous seagulls screamed at the invader.

He entered the gift shop and museum located on the first floor of the keeper's house.

Melanie, the curator and manager of the gift shop, had given him permission to go up to the platform after he told her his purpose for visiting. She hurried toward him. "Well, what do you think of our Marshall Point?"

"Amazing," Kyle said. "I'm looking for a place to stay for about a week. Do you have any suggestions?"

"If you're into the simple life, I've got a place right here. Upstairs. It's a studio apartment. One large room with kitchen and bath."

Kyle's ears perked up. "Perfect," he said.

Melanie lifted a key from a rack on the wall and said, "Follow me."

They left the gift shop and walked around the building where an outside staircase led up to the second floor. Kyle followed with ease as Melanie huffed up the steps. She unlocked the door and waved Kyle inside. He entered an open area furnished with a sofa and chair upholstered in a cozy plaid fabric. A book case filled with weighty lighthouse texts lined the wall framing a window. The desk in the corner next to a closed door provided ample space to do his work.

"This door leads to the bathroom." Melanie had followed his gaze. She walked over and opened the door. A round window in the shower area allowed plenty of light to brighten the small space. She turned and pointed to the sofa. "The couch is for sleeping. It's quite comfortable. My son used to live up here for a while." She pointed to the kitchen and said, "I know it's small, but I don't imagine you'll be doing much cooking."

"You've got that right." Kyle scanned the little apartment. He liked it. "This is perfect."

"Good. You pay by the week. Rent is a hundred bucks a week, in advance."

"It's a deal." He reached into his pocket and pulled out the money.

"Let's go downstairs, and I'll write you a receipt."

"Okay. I'll get my bag." Kyle skipped down the steps ahead of Melanie.

Kyle sat on the landing outside his front door drinking coffee. The crisp, salty air and the fabulous view of the lighthouse in front of him did little to dispel his misery. No matter how hard he tried to push Amy out of his mind, the memory of her smile, the softness of her skin and the silkiness of her hair as he ran his fingers through it haunted him still. He made up his mind. The first thing he needed to do was to go into town and buy a bottle of booze. He had no intentions of getting drunk, but a drink or two before bedtime would help him get through the night.

He retrieved the car keys and his camera and headed toward his car. He checked his watch as he glanced toward the gift shop. *She doesn't open until ten.* He was glad, because at this point he didn't want to talk to Melanie. He suspected that her bright blue, inquisitive eyes saw a lot more than he wanted her to know.

He crossed the dirt path leading to the parking lot and hopped into the rental car. He took the road leading into Port Clyde Harbor. A half a mile down the road, he passed a small cottage. An old battered jeep in need of a paint job sat on the front lawn sporting a For Sale sign. Kyle slammed on the brakes to take a closer look when the door opened, and a stocky man with balding head walked carefully down the porch steps.

"Are you interested in my jeep?"

Before Kyle could answer he continued, "It may not look so hot but the engine is in tiptop condition." He walked around to the driver's side and stretched out his hand. "Jeremiah Creeper."

Kyle scanned his face, lined and deeply tanned, and guessed him to be in his seventies. Jeremiah's squinty grey eyes regarded Kyle with curiosity.

"Kyle Weldon," he said and reached for Jeremiah's outstretched hand. The firm grip took him by surprise. "I was on my way into town," he said as he got out of the car. "I just couldn't resist a closer look. I used to own a jeep when I was younger. My first car. It got wrecked," he added with a crooked smile. He stepped closer. The excellent condition of the interior surprised him. The exterior sported a few dents, nothing serious; however, it needed a paint job.

"Are you looking for a jeep?"

Kyle shook his head. "Not really. I'm here on assignment. I've got a rental car." He pointed his head toward the vehicle.

"What do you do?" Jeremiah asked?

"I'm a photojournalist. I'm doing a story on the Marshall Point as well as some of the other lighthouses along the coast."

"Well, you don't say. Come on inside and have a cup of coffee with me." Jeremiah led him up the front porch and inside. He offered him a seat at the kitchen table and reached for the coffee pot. "I've got this going all day long," he said and poured two cups. "Milk and sugar?" he asked.

"Black for me."

Kyle took one swallow and cringed. The strong, bitter liquid made his mouth pucker. Jeremiah served a plate piled with stale oatmeal cookies. After one bite, Kyle began dunking them into the coffee. Jeremiah grinned; he dunked as well.

"How do you like our lighthouse? You know, the manner of lighting used in lighthouses has changed from large candles used in the sixth century to lamps with hollow circular wicks fueled by fish oil and later mineral or vegetable oil. Things changed drastically when the Frenchman August Fresnel invented a new type of lighting, a single light surrounded by refracting prisms that directed a concentrated beam through a large glass magnifier. Resembling a beehive in shape, it served as a much more powerful replacement of the current light source used in the towers."

Kyle listened intently, and Jeremiah continued. "I bet you don't know the pharaohs erected the first lighthouse in the harbor of Alexandria, Egypt, around 300 BC. The recent discovery of the underwater remains by a team of French archaeologists gives testimony to the splendor and size of the Pharos of Alexandria lighthouse." Jeremiah leaned back in his chair, paused significantly, then rose, and walked toward a crammed bookshelf in the adjacent living room. Reaching for a volume and pulling it out, he said, "Here, read this. I have a feeling you may find it interesting."

Kyle looked at the title, *Lighthouses of Maine.* His eyes met Jeremiah's who nodded and said, "That's what I thought. I bet you've lived in this state all your life and are aware of the lighthouses of course, but how many have you actually visited?"

"Guilty as charged, but you know what? I'm going to visit every single one of them, and I'm going to take lots of pictures."

"I bet you will. Remember you're living in the middle of God's finest creation: the sovereign State of Maine"

Kyle laughed.

"It's no laughing matter," Jeremiah chided with a grin, "It's the simple truth. As you continue to educate yourself about the history of these great beacons of hope which played such a vital role in maritime history, and still do, you can't help but develop a great respect for the courageous men who monitored the sound of the lighthouse bell, or siren, which was often the mariner's first alert to dangers in the waters. When shipwrecks occurred, the lighthouse keepers and their families often risked their lives in open rowboats to rescue sailors from turbulent waters and certain death." Jeremiah rose to fill his coffee cup. He motioned to Kyle who declined.

Sunlight streaming through the kitchen window hinted the sun had arrived at its zenith, and Kyle rose. "I've got to be on my way. Thanks for the hospitality and the book. I'll be sure to return it."

"No problem. Take your time. Come visit anytime while you're here."

———◆———

"Yeah," Luke answered the phone, munching on a chocolate chip cookie.

"Luke, is your mom at home?"

"Lisa? What a surprise. Mom is still at work," he laughed. "Looks like you've got to talk to me."

Lisa didn't answer, but he could hear her breathing.

"Let me guess, you want to hear news about Kyle," he said sarcastically and weighed the option of hanging up. He could picture her in his mind, fighting with her principles, a battle she would eventually lose.

"Luke, I was wondering…"

Ah, here it comes. He swallowed the rest of his cookie, dropping onto the kitchen chair, and propped his feet on the table.

"Yes," he said sharply. He intended to make her imminent request as difficult as he could for her.

Lisa paused briefly. He could hear her breath coming in short puffs. "I was wondering if you could give me Kyle's address," she finally said.

"Why do you want to know?"

"Well, I'm taking a few days off..." the long silence spoke volumes.

He waited, sensing what was coming, yet somehow he couldn't believe it. Why couldn't she see how much he loved her and appreciated everything about her? She probably planned to visit Kyle. Kyle, who showed no interest in her, could not care less about her, and would never love her like he, Luke, did. When she remained quiet, he finished her sentence, "and you want to pay him a visit." He heard her gasp as she struggled for control of her voice.

"Yes. I have a feeling he's going through a difficult time and needs me. Women sense these things and have a better understanding..." she rambled on.

His anger rose for a minute and then ebbed. True, he loved her and wanted her for himself, but he also cared enough to see her happy, even if the object of her affection was Kyle.

"Got a pencil?" he said and gave her the address of Marshall Point. "He stays at the keeper's house on the lighthouse grounds. I know he plans to travel up the coast a bit, so you may want to call to make sure he is at Port Clyde."

"That's okay. I want to surprise him. I'll take my chances." She could not contain the thrill in her voice. "Thank you, Luke. It was decent of you to give me Kyle's information, especially since... since..."

"Yeah, since you dumped me. Look, I still care about you, and I want to see you happy." He squared his shoulders and lifted his head. *Welcome to adulthood.* "Have a safe trip," he said and hung up.

———◆———

Kyle became engrossed in his assignment and worked late into the night, doing research for the article accompanying the photographs. The days passed quickly, but he dreaded the nights. Every time he closed his eyes, he saw Amy. One night, he got out of bed, left the apartment, and crossed the wooden bridge to the lighthouse. He climbed the stairs leading to the platform. The wind whipped and slapped him with salty sprays. He licked his lips and shuddered. Leaning over the railing, he stared at the black water speckled with bright crystal dots. He raised his head and opened his mouth in a mournful scream as he fell against the tower wall and sank to his feet. Crumpling into a sorry heap, he went to sleep.

"Ahoy there," the voice boomed through the early morning. Kyle opened his eyes. He shivered as he tried to get his bearings. He rose. Sunshine warmed his face, and the sea below rippled calmly. He looked around.

"Ahoy, Kyle."

Jeremiah stood at the base of the lighthouse. Kyle motioned him to come up.

"Ah, what a sight to behold." Inhaling deeply, Jeremiah stood next to Kyle. "Standing up here is always a humbling experience." He glanced at Kyle who remained quiet. "Did you know the light of Marshall Point was electrified in 1935, with a kerosene oil wick lamp for standby? In 1971 they completed automation and removed the Fresnel lens. The present light comes from a tiny bulb encased in a plastic lens; batteries provide a back-up electrical power source."

Kyle nodded perfunctorily and shot him a weak smile.

"Hey, are you okay? Have you spent the night up here?"

"I guess I did. I don't remember what happened."

Jeremiah rubbed his chin. The age old sounds of the sea and the gulls surrounded Marshall Point and the two men standing on its platform.

"I need to get my act together, Jeremiah. I've got everything going for me, yet..." Without finishing the sentence Kyle stared out at the ocean.

"Hmm, is it a woman?"

"Yes."

Kyle's fists clenched and opened. "I love her," he finally said, "but she's no good. She played me, and I was too stupid to notice."

"Come," Jeremiah turned to leave the platform. Kyle remained still as he stared out at the sea. "Come," Jeremiah stretched out his arm. "I'll treat you to breakfast at Lucky's Diner."

Kyle turned and said. "Thanks, but I need a shower and a shave." He managed a crooked grin. "I'm a mess."

"I'll wait for you. Let's go." Jeremiah led the way down the steps and across the bridge with Kyle following slowly behind him.

"Go ahead and do your thing. I'll talk to Melanie for a spell." Jeremiah entered the gift shop and Kyle climbed the steps to his apartment, dragging his feet all the way up. His head pounded, and this stomach made nauseous rumbles. Maybe some food would help him feel better.

After his shower, he dressed and picked up his wallet and keys. His cell phone buzzed.

"Hello."

"Kyle." Her voice raised, his mom spoke quickly. "Lisa is on her way to see you. Luke tried to dissuade her, but she wouldn't hear of it. She said she had a feeling you needed her."

Lisa was coming to Marshall Point. That's the last thing he wanted right now. She'll look at him with her inquisitive eyes and sense his misery. "Mom, I'm very busy. I don't have time for her," he yelled. "I'll be travelling up the coast and may not be here when she arrives."

"Luke told her all that. She made reservations at a bed and breakfast in Port Clyde. She plans to stay a couple of days. She said she needed a vacation…"

"Mom, this is not a good time," he interrupted her impatiently.

"There is never a good time for you to see Lisa, that's obvious. Anyway, I wanted to let you know. Have fun," she said crisply and hung up.

The dial tone buzzed in Kyle's ear as he stared at the phone. His mom's annoyance did not escape him. He would have to make it up to her. A knock on the door roused him.

"Ready?" Jeremiah opened the door and poked his head inside.

"Yes," Kyle rushed toward him. "I had a phone call."

Jeremiah regarded him expectantly.

"My mom. Nothing important." He didn't look at Jeremiah as he spoke.

CHAPTER 19

———◆———

THE NEXT MORNING KYLE ROSE early. After a quick cup of coffee and some toast, he grabbed his gear and stepped outside. He shivered as the cold air engulfed him. The late fall temperatures had dropped to thirty during the last couple of nights, and unless the sun showed its face, this day promised to be a cold one. He hurried back inside and reached for the lined windbreaker draped across the kitchen chair. He slipped into it and proceeded down the stairs. The silence was incredible except for the surf pounding the shore and the ever-present, screaming seagulls foraging the beach.

He unlocked the car in a hurry. He had to be gone before Lisa arrived. Maybe if she found him absent, she'd turn around and go home. There was no way he could see her or look into her probing eyes. She'd realize what a wreck he was in a minute. He didn't want her pity. What was wrong with her anyhow, driving up here to spy on him, after he had made it clear to her he wasn't interested in a relationship? Although he had to admit, Lisa would never act the way Amy had. He got into the car and reached for the map. Bass Harbor Head Light was located on Mount Desert Island, a two and a half hours' drive.

The trip took him through incredible landscapes. He stopped often and took pictures. He agreed with Jeremiah, the beauty of Maine was unsurpassed. He arrived at Acadia National Park three hours later, parked the car and looked up. The sky was crystal clear, and he headed for the lighthouse.

The stunning cliffside setting of Bass Harbor Head lighthouse on Mount Desert Island made it easily one of the most photographed lighthouses in New England. The 32-foot cylindrical tower was built in 1858 to mark the entrance to Blue Hill Bay and to guide vessels making their way into Bass Harbor. The light was equipped with a fourth-order Fresnel lens, which emitted a red flash every four seconds. The steep rock face location offered several vantage points. Kyle had researched the light house extensively, thanks to Jeremiah's book. He'd learned the tides could vary considerably here, and the angle of the sun, relative to the horizon and the ocean side of the lighthouse, changes widely depending on the season of the year.

He stood in awe as his eyes scaled the tower. He took many photos covering all angles and then followed the path leading to a set of steps down the front face of the cliff, eventually arriving at a prime spot for capturing an incredible view of the lighthouse and the cliffs. He turned and took in the rugged and unpredictable Maine coast with its roughness, loose stones, and slippery spots. Smacked by recurrent chilly gusts, he stood for a long time soaking up the fabulous view. At this point, he was the only visitor standing between the cliff and the sea. The solitude offered him comfort and eased his pain. He heard voices. People approached, and he refocused his mind on the task at hand and climbed the staircase to the top.

Not far north of the light was a geological wonder—the only fjord on the East coast of North America and carved during the last glacial period. Jeremiah had urged him not to miss it, and when he arrived, he was glad he took the extra time to visit the fjord.

On the way back to Marshall Point, he grabbed a sandwich at a diner. It occurred to him that Lisa may have shown up, only to discover he was gone. Maybe she'd turn around and go home, leaving him alone to wallow in his misery, although, remarkably, the oppressing sense of sadness had lifted.

He pulled into the parking area just as Melanie locked up shop for the day. She waved. "Kyle, a young lady stopped by to see you. She said she's an old friend from high school."

Kyle flinched.

"I told her you were gone for the day. She's got a place in town and will call you later. She's a mighty pretty little thing."

"That's Lisa. We're casual friends, nothing else."

Melanie studied his face. *What a shame.* Melanie liked Lisa immediately. She'd be a good match for Kyle who seemed mighty lonely and downright miserable at times

"Well, I'll be on my way. See you tomorrow." She turned, walked toward her car, and stopped. "By the way, how did you like Desert Island and our Bass Harbor Light?"

"Splendid! I must have taken a hundred pictures."

"Good. I look forward to seeing them in a magazine someday."

Kyle shook his head. "I'm afraid not. They will be part of an article I'm doing on Marshall Point for the *Portland Journal.* Bass Harbor Light deserves an article by itself explaining the beauty of the entire area."

Melanie smiled and got into her car. He watched her leave and proceeded to go up the steps to his apartment, but changed his mind and walked across the bridge to Marshall Point. He climbed the stairs leading to the platform. The dusk had deepened to near darkness, and a waning moon climbed above the flat Eastern horizon. The ever present wind squalls whipped his body. He had not meant to think of her, but it was as though Amy walked across the sea and stood in front of him blocking out the moonlight and refused to go away. Throwing her head back, she began to laugh hysterically. He covered his face. *Go away. Go away.*

"Kyle."

He turned, listening. Someone was climbing the stairs.

"Kyle." Lisa stepped onto the platform. "There you are."

He looked at her unable to speak. There was a long brittle silence, and he closed his eyes, trying to deal with this unexpected development. "Lisa…what are you doing here?" he finally said.

"I'm taking a little vacation, and I thought I'd stop by to see you…"

When he didn't answer, she added, "I was here earlier and the lady at…"

"Yes, yes. Melanie," he said impatiently. "She told me you were here."

She stepped next to him and scanned the calm sea. Shafts of moonlight ignited the surf. The wind had slowed a little. "How beautiful," she whispered, "and peaceful."

He glanced at her, barely making out her face in the dark. Somehow her presence wasn't offensive, and having her standing here next to him was strangely comforting. To be able to share this beautiful moment with someone was a new experience, and he liked it.

They stood in silence. Lisa's sense of apprehension ebbed, and she began to relax. Just to be near him caused her eyes to blur with tears of happiness. He hadn't sent her away. Maybe he was glad to see her. She craned her neck.

He chuckled and said, "You can't see too much in the dark. You have to come up here in the daytime to fully appreciate the view."

"I'd love to. Do you have time tomorrow morning? I could drive up after breakfast…and stay for a little while, but then I have to go back home."

"Going back home tomorrow?" He repeated after her, relieved. "Why don't you come for breakfast?" He hadn't planned on inviting her, but the words escaped before he could stop them.

"You cook?"

"Yes, I've been on my own for a while now and have had to learn quite a few things."

"I bet you have," her laughter rang clear through the night. "Okay, I'll be here at eight o'clock sharp."

"You're on." He saw her shiver and added, "Let's go back to the house. I'll show you my apartment." He casually took her hand and led her down the steps and across the bridge.

"I love this place, Kyle." They sat at the small kitchen table. All he could offer her was water, and she was fine with it. He looked at her face. He'd always known she was beautiful and could have any guy she wanted, so why did she choose him?

Her lids dropped and she blushed. He said quickly, "So, how's it going? What are you up to these days?"

"I'm working at the daycare center and going to college at night to get my master's in child care."

"Wow, you must be quite busy."

"Yes, but I don't mind. I love what I do. But tell me about you."

Relaxed, he leaned back and began telling her about his assignments with the paper, his trip to South Dakota and the Photo Exhibit at Quentin's Studio. He never mentioned Amy.

"Your mom told me she had been to see you. Congratulations on your success, Kyle. There was never any doubt in my mind you'd become an excellent photojournalist. It's what you wanted to do ever since you were little."

"I have a long way to go, but I've been fortunate." He paused. "I've had some breaks," he added bitterly.

She sensed the swing in his mood and said, "You'll achieve whatever you intend to. There's no doubt in my mind." She looked at her watch. "It's after midnight," she said and rose. "I've got to go and get some sleep." She stretched out her hand. "Good night, Kyle. I enjoyed this evening very much."

"So did I." He grabbed her hand, then pulled her close and gave her a hug. He walked her to the car. The surf broke upon the rocky coast in foamy crests. A mild salty breeze swept across them. She got into the car and started the engine. "See you tomorrow," she said with a quick wave and left. He stood for a long time staring after her. She had felt good in his arms. He almost didn't want to let her go.

CHAPTER 20

"KYLE." HE TURNED TO HIS side. Amy lay next to him. She leaned over and kissed him deeply. "Kyle, I love you," she whispered. He reached for her, but she was gone. He bolted up in bed and checked his watch: two a.m. "Damn," he muttered and fell back onto the pillow. He tossed and turned, but sleep evaded him completely. Finally, he jumped out of bed and padded across the room. The whiskey bottle was half empty when he lifted it to his mouth. He brought it down and looked at it. No sense in stopping now, he thought and emptied the bottle. He dropped onto a chair and closed his eyes as the spirits warmed his body. His head fell to his chest and he began to snore.

A knock on the door roused him. Sunlight filtered through the sheer curtains and he cursed. Another knock forced him to rise, and just before he opened the door, he realized, he was naked. "Just a minute," he yelled, and slipped into his pants. He opened the door and squinted.

"Morning, Kyle." Lisa stood before him wearing a pair of jeans and sweater, smiling and looking happy. He cringed inwardly. He felt horrible.

The smile on her face faded. "Did you forget? You invited me for breakfast." Her eyes scanned his face, and she saw the shadow of a beard and his mussed hair falling across his forehead. "I guess this isn't a good time," she said and turned to leave. He quickly grabbed her arm and pulled her inside.

"I'm sorry, Lisa, I overslept. Have a seat. It takes me a little time to wake up. I'm usually grouchy in the morning. I'll be right back." He disappeared into the bathroom.

She watched him leave and then she noticed the empty whiskey bottle. She bit her lip as she struggled with her emotions. She realized he was in pain. Why, she could only guess. She saw the coffee pot on the counter. "Do you mind if I make the coffee?" she called out to him.

"Go ahead. Coffee is in the cabinet above the stove." Kyle turned on the shower.

Fifteen minutes later he appeared freshly shaven, hair combed and fully dressed. "I could smell the coffee in the shower."

As she rose and filled a cup for him, her eyes met his.

"Black for me," he said.

"I need some cream."

"There's creamer in the pantry." He stood next to her, reached up to retrieve it from the cabinet, and handed it to her. "Lisa," he began but hesitated and stared at the floor.

"Look, Kyle. Why don't you let me fix breakfast for you, and then we can talk."

"Okay." He walked over to the table and sat onto the chair. He watched her quietly while she fried eggs and some ham she had located in the refrigerator. The smell of the ham tickled his nose and he realized he was starving. She worked quietly. He rose, popped bread into the toaster and began to set the table.

"This was excellent." Kyle refilled his coffee cup and looked at Lisa.

"No, thanks, I'm quite full."

"You make a hell of a breakfast."

"I have some good qualities you don't know about," she said shyly.

He smiled. "I know you better than you think."

"Maybe you do, but…"

"Lisa," he interrupted her, "something has happened. I've met a woman…"

"You don't have to tell me, Kyle, especially if it's painful to talk about it."

"It is… very painful, but I want to tell you about her," he paused. "Yes, strangely, I want to talk about her – with you."

She nodded, all the while trying to control her rapid heartbeat. As he collected his thoughts, she said a silent prayer, *please don't let me screw this up and say the wrong thing, and he'll hate me forever.*

Kyle told her all about Amy, how they met, and how she was instrumental in getting him the job at the paper. He talked for a long time and she just listened. She began to relax, and her heart went out to him. She of all people could relate to his pain. She wondered what this woman looked like. He said she was beautiful. At this moment Lisa hated Amy with every fiber of her being, yet, thanks to Amy's infidelities, she was able to sit here with Kyle in this intimate moment as he shared his story with her.

When he was finished he said, "That's it. The saga of my love affair with Amy." He managed a twisted smile as he rose, "And you're the only one who knows all the gory details." He walked over to the counter and refilled his cup. When he turned, she had joined him.

"I'm sorry, Kyle…"

"Don't be sorry for me, Lisa. I was a fool. She duped me, I acted like a naïve school boy, falling for her the way I did."

She stood in silence. Being close to him made all her anxieties disappear. She was blissfully happy, fully alive, and wanted to remember this moment forever.

She glanced at her watch. "I've got to go." she whispered.

He put his hands on her shoulders and looked into her eyes. "I'm glad you came, Lisa. I didn't think I would ever be able to talk to anyone about Amy. You made it easy, and I thank you for that." He bent down and kissed her on the cheek.

She lifted her hands and cupped his face. "I love you," she said without pausing, "I love you more than you'll ever know." She kissed him on the mouth, grabbed her purse, and dashed out the door.

He stood stunned and then raced after her. She was already backing out of the parking space.

"Lisa wait," he called out and ran to the driver's side. "Wait…" his breath came hard. She lowered the window. There were tears in her eyes, and he reached over to wipe them with the back of his hand.

"Lisa, I want to see you again. I should wrap up my assignment here in a few days. I'll be back in Portland soon. Let's get together then."

She gave him a huge smile and said, "You know where to reach me. Bye, Kyle." She hit the gas pedal, and the car took off.

He stood for a long time staring at the road. A strong squall pelted his back and he walked down to the shore. The sea swelled in broad billows that melted into one another. He sat on the rocks while Marshall Point, on his left, stood guard.

"Morning, Kyle." Melanie had arrived to open the gift shop. "How are you this breezy morning?"

He rose and walked toward her. "Just great."

"Yes, I can tell by that look on your face something has changed."

He laughed. "You see right through me. How do you do that?"

"Intuition," she said. "You look a little bit happy this morning. I'm glad."

"You mean I didn't look happy before?"

"No. Absolutely miserable. I was getting worried about you."

"Well, you can stop worrying. I'll be all right." He waved and headed up the stairs.

"About time, my boy," she muttered and dug in her purse for the keys.

Joan was sweeping the front porch when Lisa's car pulled into the driveway. Her gaze flicked upward. Luke had told her about Lisa's plan to visit Kyle, and she feared it had not gone well for Lisa. Joan walked down the steps just as Lisa got out of the car. Joan noticed the smile on her face and the swing in her step as Lisa rushed toward her.

"Oh, Mrs. Weldon, I just had to stop by." Lisa took Joan's arm and pulled her over to the steps. They sat and Lisa said, "Did you know I went to see Kyle?"

"Yes, Luke told me. How did it go?" Joan studied Lisa's face. She absolutely glowed.

"Oh, Mrs. Weldon, I'm so glad I decided to visit him. I now know that Kyle loves me."

Joan stiffened.

"We had a wonderful time together. He told me everything. He's been so unhappy, but now he has me. He just doesn't know it yet."

"Doesn't know what?"

Lisa turned to her. "That he loves me, of course." She leaned back and smiled with contentment. "And once he finds out, we'll be together. Forever."

"That's a long time." Joan failed to hide the irony in her voice.

Lisa put her arm around Joan. "Mrs. Weldon, aren't you happy for us?"

Joan straightened up. "Look Lisa," she said firmly. "I would like nothing more than for you and Kyle to be together. You know how fond I am of you, but I fear…"

"Don't fear. Everything's okay." Lisa jumped up. "Gotta go. Don't want to be late for work." She pulled Joan to her feet and twirled her around. "I'm so happy." She kissed the older woman on the check and ran toward her car. "Bye."

Joan raised her hand in farewell as she watched the dented blue Camry leave the driveway.

CHAPTER 21

⬩

THE WIND SCREAMED IN THE trees. Clumps of snow dropped on the roof of the lean-to. Kyle opened his eyes and reality hit him. He rose and peered through the crack in the door. Fractions of sky visible through the tree tops revealed a heavy cloud cover. Snow fell steadily, whipped into frenzy by powerful gusts. He squinted as he checked his watch: 11:00 A.M. He paced the floor, then paused, and leaning against the door, he closed his eyes. No matter how hard he tried, he could not dispel the memory of Melanie's body, and the pool of blood on the floor. He began pacing again and then stopped in front of the bucket to relieve himself.

A door slammed and footsteps scrunched through the snow. The lock rattled, the door opened, and without saying a word, the man tossed a plastic bag inside, shut the door, and left.

"Wait," Kyle called after him. "Come back. I need to talk to you." There was no reply, and he hammered the rough wood with his fists. He sank into a squat and his head fell onto his chest. Fear invaded his mind. *I don't want to die. I'm too young to die. I have too much to do yet. My career is just getting off the ground. There are many pictures to take, stories to write, get married... Get married?* Amy's beautiful face rose in front of him and slowly turned into a sneer as she threw back her head and laughed cruelly. The image faded, and he thought of Lisa. Kind, gentle Lisa. She would be the girl he would marry if he ever got out of here. He picked up the bag. Inside was a loaf of bread, a jar of peanut butter, a bottle of water, and a plastic spoon. He found, despite his anger and despair, he was famished. He unscrewed the peanut butter jar and using the spoon handle fixed a double decker sandwich. He ate with gusto, drinking from the bottle in between bites. When he was finished he fixed another sandwich. Peanut butter had never tasted this good. Sitting on the cot his head dropped, and he rolled onto his side and fell asleep.

The chill in the room woke him. He pulled the blanket tighter when he realized the fire was in embers. He fed the stove. Sparks exploded and flames licked the wood. He shut the gate and crawled back onto the cot.

Light crept through the cracks in the door, projecting ever-changing patterns on the floor. Kyle opened his eyes. The wind had subsided. He yawned and saw his breath escaping into the air. Then the cold hit him. The fire was out. He scrambled out of bed and yanked the gate open. Nothing but cold ashes. He scooped them into the empty bag that held the food. He rose and was wiping his face with his arm, when the smell hit his nose. He needed a wash and a shave and, above all, a change of clothes. He realized none of these things were in his immediate future. He wrapped the blanket around him, banged on the door, and yelled as loudly as he could, "Hey. HEY! I need wood and matches." It took about an hour of erratic screaming that left him horse before the door opened just enough to allow more wood and a book of matches being pushed inside.

"You're one stupid boy. I told you to watch the fire. Next time I'll let you freeze to death." The door slammed.

"No, you won't." Kyle stood next to the closed door.

The rattling of keys stopped, and the man said, "Oh yeah? Why not?"

"Obviously you have plans, and me being dead is not part of any of them."

"You're right about that." The man chortled and shuffled back to the cabin.

Joan's eyes flew open. She thought she heard the doorbell. She turned her head to check the clock on the night table, six A.M. It must have been a dream. She rolled over on her stomach and pulled up the covers. Here it was again. Persistent, demanding. Someone kept his thumb on the button. She jumped out of bed, angry and worried at the same time. Something must be wrong. Slipping into her robe, and slippers, she hurried out the door and down the steps.

She opened the front door and stood facing two men dressed in trench coats. She glanced beyond their heads and saw the police cruiser parked in the driveway. Her heartbeat sped up when one of them said, "Sorry to bother you at this hour Ma'am. I'm Officer McNamara and this here," he pointed to the other man, "is my partner Officer Wiseshul." They produced ID batches. "May we come in? We need to talk to you about your son."

"Luke is upstairs, asleep," she said and stepped aside to allow them to enter.

"Is Kyle Weldon your son, Ma'am? "

"Why, yes. He's not here He's in Port Clyde Harbor on assignment."

The men looked at her suspiciously. "Are you sure? Have you seen him or talked to him during the last 24 hours?" Officer McNamara asked.

"Yes, I'm sure. I've not talked to him during the last 24 hours, but I called him last week, and he told me he was going to visit Marshall Point Light to do a story. No wait, I spoke with him again about four days ago."

The men remained silent. Her face turned ashen. Something had happened to Kyle. "What's wrong? Is my son all right?" Fear knotted inside her. When they still didn't answer, she demanded, "What has happened to Kyle?"

Officer Wiseshul said, "He has disappeared." He glanced at the other man and then added, "He is a suspect in the killing of the proprietor of the Marshall Point Gift Shop and Museum."

Joan's jaw dropped. She crept to a nearby chair and fell into it. "Murder," she whispered.

"Mom, what's wrong?" Luke stood on the landing. "Who are these men?" He ran down the stairs and moved next to Joan who had brought up her hands and covered her face. "What do you want with my mom? Why are you upsetting her?"

Before they could answer he headed for the phone. "I'm calling the police."

"No, Luke, no." Joan rose from the chair. "These men *are* the police."

"Police? What do you want with us?"

Joan answered for them, "They're looking for Kyle. Apparently he's disappeared. They're accusing him of having killed someone in Port Clyde Harbor."

"Kyle, a killer?" Luke exclaimed. "No way."

The men turned to leave. One of them handed her a business card. "If you hear from your son, you must notify us immediately." He opened the front door hesitated and added, "If he gets in touch with you, I strongly suggest you urge him to turn himself in. Goodbye, Ma'am."

They left. Luke slammed the door behind them.

CHAPTER 22

———————

"HELLO."

"Mrs. Weldon, it's Lisa." Her hand shook as she held a copy of the *Graceville Register*. *"LOCAL MAN SUSPECTED OF MURDER,"* the headline screamed.

"I guess you've heard." Joan tried unsuccessfully to stem the flow of tears. She had been crying all morning.

"I'm looking at the article in the paper right now. I know with absolute certainty Kyle is innocent."

"Tell that to the police," Joan said bitterly. "There's a statewide search for Kyle going on. For all we know, he could be dead…"

"Don't say that," Lisa interjected. "What if he walked in on a robbery at the gift shop and got kidnapped?"

Joan didn't answer.

"It could have happened that way," Lisa insisted.

"They're looking for him. The woman was killed two days ago. I fear Kyle's dead also."

"He's not dead."

Joan choked on her tears. She reached for a tissue and blew her nose while Lisa waited impatiently. "I don't want to believe he's dead," Joan said between sniffles, "but there is that possibility. I'm just being realistic."

"I'm going to Port Clyde Harbor."

"Lisa, it's a crime scene. They won't let you go anywhere near the museum."

"Well, I can't just sit around here and do nothing while Kyle's in trouble."

"We must let the police do their job." Joan released a labored sigh. "The officers told me they'll keep me posted. If I hear anything, I'll call you immediately."

"Please, promise you'll get in touch with me right away once you get any news. Promise me."

"I promise. Bye, Lisa."

Kyle jogged the floor. Thirteen feet. Back and forth. He had to find a way to freedom or face certain death. Despite the fact that the guy kept his face covered. Kyle knew most kidnap victims didn't survive. He would be a loose end, one capable of helping the cops. He stopped at the door and pressed his eye against the crack. It was snowing again. Impulsively, he turned to check the stove. The blazing fire fussed and snapped. He walked to the middle of the room and fell onto his hands. He did thirty push-ups, and then proceeded into the bridge position, a yoga pose he had watched Amy do. He continued employing several other poses. He'd made fun of Amy, but found the poses relaxing. Soon he began to yawn. He jumped up and walked over to the cot. He had two more slices of bread left. The peanut butter was gone. He guzzled down the bread and then stretched out on the primitive cot. Funny, it became more comfortable every day. His lids dropped.

A cold blast of air hit his face, and he groped for the blanket. He blinked. The door was wide open, and the man stood pointing a shotgun at Kyle. He kicked the bag on the floor toward Kyle. "Here's your grub. Guess what's on the menu today." He laughed out loud. He sniffed the air. "It stinks in here," he said and turned his head toward the overflowing bucket.

"Let me empty it," Kyler begged.

The man contemplated that thought and said, "I guess that'll be all right. Remember, no funny business." He pointed the gun at the bucket and then back at Kyle.

Kyle held his breath as he carried the bucket outside. He dumped the contents into nearby bushes while surreptitiously surveying his surroundings. He guessed the distance between the front porch of the cabin and the shed entrance to be about 25 feet. The jeep, parked in front of the cabin, had been cleared of snow, a sign it had been moved not long ago.

"Hurry up." The man poked the gun in his side. "Hey, wait a minute." He reached for Kyle's right hand and in one quick swoop removed the watch.

Kyle made a move toward him. "Don't even try it," the man growled. "I've got nothing to lose. I'll shoot you dead and let you rot here in the wilderness." He pushed Kyle toward the door and then gave him a swift kick in the behind. Kyle fell forward on top of the bucket, and the man slammed the door and locked it. "That's a good looking watch. Must've paid a pretty penny for it." The voice faded away.

Moments later, Kyle heard the engine start as the tires crunched through the snow, and then there was silence. He looked at his empty wrist. He wouldn't miss the watch, a gift from Amy. He was only sorry that now he'd lose track of time, and had to find other means to count the days. It occurred to him, he hadn't thought about Amy all day. He tried to conjure up her face in his mind. All he got was a faded image, and he took that to be a good sign. Reaching for the bag on the floor, he looked inside. More bread and a full jar of peanut butter. *If I ever get out of here, I'll never want to even look at peanut butter.* Crossing his legs on the cot, he leaned back against the wall. Hands jammed into armpits, he closed his eyes. So much had happened he needed to process. He must come up with a plan of escape before.... He shook his head. *I don't want to think too far ahead.* He splayed his hands out wide to stretch and then relaxing them and dropping them into his lap. *Mom and Luke must know by now that I have disappeared. I bet she's worried, and Luke too.* He knew

Luke had a crush on Lisa. But he also knew his brother loved him nevertheless. Lisa, the girl he cast carelessly aside. Inexplicably, Lisa's image had replaced Amy's and he found himself thinking about her a lot. *Once I get out of here....* The question was would be survive this ordeal, or in the end, be shot and left to rot as the man had threatened? Sorrow tied a huge painful knot inside him. He thought about the many mistakes he made in his short life. An ambition that drove him away from home, discarding old friends, and then he allowed himself to become ensnared by an opportunist who exploited his naiveté. *Yes, Amy, you used me. And I foolishly believed I was in love with you.* He had the time and focus to see everything so clearly now.

Kyle heard an engine approach and the sound of the handbrake pulled into place. The door slammed. He held his breath. Footsteps clumped up the steps to the cabin, and he relaxed. His eyes searched the crack in the door. Darkness had spread across the snow. He rose and fed the stove. *Might as well go to sleep.*

CHAPTER 23

———◆———

RICHARD SLOAN SAT AT HIS desk. Again, he flipped through the photographs of Marshall Point Lighthouse taken from all angles, the quaint town of Port Clyde Harbor, the beautiful, rugged coastline. He came to picture of a woman standing in front of the museum at Marshall Point. She smiled—a warm, friendly smile—her right arm holding a bunch of wild roses growing in abundance along the Maine seashore. Richard noticed Kyle had taken several photos of Melanie. *Kyle, what happened? I'll never believe you killed that woman. I only hope and pray you are still alive.* He picked up the phone and dialed Joan's number.

She answered after the first ring.

"Mrs. Weldon, Richard Sloan here." When she didn't answer he added, "From the *Portland Journal.*"

"Yes, of course." She didn't even try to conceal her disappointment. "How are you?" she said lamely.

"Mrs. Weldon, the police dropped off some photos Kyle had taken for his assignment."

"Is there any news about him? Oh, please tell me, is he alive?" The words tumbled out.

"Kyle's camera was discovered in a pawnshop in Bangor. The fool who stole it was either ignorant about cameras, or he forgot to remove the memory card. The police department printed the photos and gave me copies."

Fear and anger knotted inside her. "Why didn't they contact me?"

"I suppose, they will eventually. I want you to know, I hired a private investigator. He'll get in touch with you to garner some information." He heard her cry softly, and an incredible sadness swept over him. He was so fond of Kyle. He could have been the son he never had, and he knew deep in his gut that Kyle did not kill the woman. The truth had to be sought and once discovered, Kyle would be cleared.

"Thank you, Mr. Sloan. I appreciate all you're doing." Sobs caught in Joan's throat and she said, "I'll do whatever you want me to. Anything. My son is not a murderer."

"I know that, Mrs. Weldon. I'll keep in touch. Goodbye." He hung up just as the door opened. Amy walked into his office and dropped onto the chair opposite his desk.

"Any news?" She spoke with a laconic drawl. He watched her and shook his head. Every time he saw her lately she had been drinking.

"They found Kyle's camera in a pawnshop," he said.

"Shah…" she looked at him, her eyes unfocused. Her head wobbled and then dropped. She began to snore.

His hand reached up and he gently pushed her hair away from her face and kissed her on the forehead. *My darling daughter, you've lost your way. Why won't you let me help you? I love you so much.* He caressed her chin. How much her beauty reminded him of his wife, yet their personalities differed starkly. Maybe if her mother had lived…he straightened up. No sense dwelling on ifs and buts. Life is what it is, and Amy made her own choices. He had tried to talk to her so many times, but she rejected anything he said. He grabbed his coat, turned off the light, and left the office.

Walking down the hallway he stopped at Conley's open door.

"Richard, got a minute?" Conley said.

He stepped into Conley's office, and he handed him a copy of the front page. GRACEVILLE MAN SUSPECTED IN KILLING, the headline shouted. He sighed heavily.

"We couldn't hold off any longer," Conley said.

"Yes, I know." Richard flung the paper onto the desk. "I still don't believe that boy did it."

"I know. The truth will come out. Maybe he'll come forward now and explain..."

"If he's able," Richard interjected and left.

Kyle sat on the cot. He couldn't sleep. Maybe some exercise would help. He proceeded with his regular routine: push-ups, knee bends and several yoga poses, ending with running in place. He stopped when he heard footsteps. He held his breath as he stood and waited. The door opened and the man flung pieces of wood at him, along with the usual plastic bag containing bread, and peanut butter. The door slammed shut.

"Wait," Kyle kicked at the door. "Come back. I need to empty the bucket."

The lock rattled and the door flung open, and Kyle jumped the man. He had managed to get hold of his neck, but to no avail. The man flexed his arms. He spun around and his powerful punch landed on Kyle's jaw. He dropped on his back, only inches from the burning stove. When he gained consciousness, he lay sprawled on top of the wood; the taste of blood invaded his mouth. He sat up and grimaced when he moved his jaw. Wiping his chin with the shirtsleeve, he realized the blood had already dried. *I must have been out for quite a while. I should have hit him with a piece of wood. I should have... but I didn't. Better luck next time.* He dragged himself over to the cot, crawled beneath the blanket and went to sleep.

The next morning a storm had moved in pounding the shed with unrelenting gales. The narrow strip of grey light seeping through the crack revealed a gray, angry sky. Kyle remained on the cot staring at the ceiling. How long had he been here? He'd lost all track of time. When the man stole his watch, Kyle had planned to design some way to keep count of the days, but he never got around to it. Why not? He didn't have anything else to do. He turned on his stomach and buried his face in the mattress. What was wrong with him? He couldn't give up. He'd read about kidnappings and seen movies, in which the hero always managed to escape. It seemed so easy. *Grow up, Kyle. This is the real world. Stop feeling sorry for yourself. No one is coming to the rescue.* He released a bitter laugh. *Hell, no one knows where I am.* He jumped up. The room spun around him, and he fell back on the cot. He was hungry and thirsty, but somehow he didn't have the energy to feed himself. He closed his eyes.

CHAPTER 24

———◆———

NO MATTER HOW HARD SHE tried, pictures of Kyle popped into her mind. Kyle on the run, Kyle hiding in empty buildings, Kyle wielding a gun. "No," she cried and her head dropped on her arms.

"Joan," Vince Rappel rushed into the room. He hesitated and then gently put his arm on her shoulder. "Joan," he said, "why don't you go home? This stuff can wait. Go home and take care of yourself."

She raised her head. It hurt him to look into her tear streaked face.

"No Vince, I want to stay. I need…" She began to shake as the fearful images invaded her consciousness again.

His arm tightened, "Shhh. Of course you can stay. Do what you think best. I want to help you in any way I can."

"You are, Vince. You are. This job is good for me, especially now." She wiped her face with her hand, and he handed her a tissue. "Thanks." She managed a faint smile. "My bookkeeping skills have not deserted me, it seems."

"Oh, I'm not worried. I knew you'd do a great job." He straightened up and looked at her with gentle eyes. "I love having you around, you know that."

Joan blinked and smiled, "Yes, I do."

"Mr. Rappel," a knock on the door dispelled the magic of the moment.

"Come in," Vince barked.

One of the busboys entered, followed by the same two police officers who had visited Joan a week ago.

"Good afternoon." They turned to Joan and gave a slight bow.

"Mrs. Weldon, we stopped at your house, and your son, Luke, directed us here. We've got news about Kyle," one of the men said.

She shot out of her chair. "Where is he? Is he all right?" She ran around the desk and stopped a foot from the investigator.

"We don't know. We assume he's okay. Richard Sloan from the *Portland Journal* received a ransom-note for Kyle."

"Ransom-note? Doesn't that mean he did nothing wrong?"

"Maybe. We can't be certain."

"But surely ransom is only collected for a person who's still alive." She paused, and then her eyes opened wide, and she exclaimed, "Now you know he *is* innocent." She looked at the men triumphantly and added, "And he is alive."

"Well, your son is still a suspect, but now we have something to go on." He showed her a copy of the ransom-note. She took it from his hand. Crudely fashioned in cut letters it said 'If you want Kyle Weldon alive pay $250,000.00 in small bills when notified as to where and when.'

"Oh my God," Joan swayed and Vince caught her. He led her to the couch in the corner and hurried for the kitchen. He returned shortly with a glass of water. "Here, drink this," he said kindly.

She brushed him away and rose. "I don't have that kind of money."

"The ransom-note is addressed to Richard Sloan, Ma'am. We don't encourage paying ransom," one of the officers said. "You let us handle the matter."

"I have to think about that." She raised her small hand balled into a fist, "Now that you know Kyle's innocent, I want his name cleared." The anger in her voice reflected in her flushed cheeks and blazing eyes.

"Of course. We'll be in touch. Goodbye, Ma'am." They turned to Vince, "Sir," and left.

Vince walked into the other room and picked-up Joan's purse. He lifted her coat from the clothes tree and held it for her. "Look," he said, "I want you to call it a day. Go home, take a long bath, and try to relax."

She kept shaking her head as she slipped into her coat. "How can I relax? My son is accused of murder, he's disappeared, and now this news about a ransom. I have to sell my house, and still it won't be enough money to pay it." She turned to him. "Tell me, how can I relax?"

He led her to the door. "You've got to try," he said patiently. "There's no other choice. You must go on about your routine and above all take care of yourself. Let the police handle the matter for now. This ordeal may take a long time."

Her head dropped. "I can't," she said. "I simply can't."

His arm draped around her shoulders, and he steered her out of the room. "I'm taking you home," he said.

Neill leaned across the counter, the *Portland Journal* in front of him. The breakfast crowd had left, time to take a little break. He poured himself another cup of coffee and proceeded to read the paper. A man entered the café and took a seat at the counter.

Neill looked up.

"Coffee, black," the man said. He opened a newspaper and began reading it. Neill filled a mug and placed it in front of him.

"I know that boy," Neill said and pointed to Kyle's photo on the front page.

The man didn't seem interested. Neill studied his face. He liked to assess people by their appearance, but this one was difficult. He was African-American with long furrows in his forehead and cheeks, but his hazel eyes flashed brightly. Morgan Freeman came to Neill's mind. Yes, there was a powerful resemblance.

Turning the page, the man pushed the empty mug toward Neill who refilled it. The man kept reading the article, while Neill remained silent. Finally, he moved the paper aside.

"So you know this guy?" he said. "Why don't you tell me a little about him?"

Neill felt a certain kinship with Kyle and was only too happy to oblige. He began to tell Kyle's story as he knew it. When he was finished, he straightened up and said, "This boy is no killer, trust me. I know people. I get an education here."

The man rose and pulled out a business card. He handed it to Neill and said, "If you can remember anything else, please get in touch with me." He threw ten dollars onto the counter and left.

"So long…" the words faded as Neill read the card: Gareth Morton, Private Investigator.

"Well I'll be…" Neill's face turned into a grin. "I hope you'll find Kyle." He tacked the card to the cork bulletin board attached to the wall next to the front door.

The cell phone rang, and the man flipped it open.

"How's it going?" a rough voice bellowed into his ear.

"Swell. The ransom note has been delivered. I'm getting ready to let them know where to drop off the loot. How are things up there?"

"Cold as hell. I'm freezing my ass off. We need to wrap this up quick."

"It should all be taken care of in the next day. You make sure you get across the border and wait for me. I'll get there as soon as I can." He disconnected and climbed into the jeep.

The jeep rumbled down the icy path. The man cursed as the wheels spun and he nearly slammed into a tree. *Must be careful.* Soon he'd be on the main road, which should be in better shape. He checked Kyle's watch. She was a beauty. He'd read the inscription: To Kyle from Amy. It would bring a good bit at the pawnshop, but he didn't dare to go back to where he pawned the camera equipment. Although there was the inscription, it would take a while for the cops to connect the dots. Cops were slow and stupid and he was just too smart. Besides once he got the ransom money, he'd be off to Canada and then some remote and warmer place.

The brakes screeched and the vehicle came to a stop at the edge of the road. The engine had stalled, and he peered out the window. The side of the mountain dropped straight down. He gazed across distant tree tops, their branches low under the heavy snow. He sat still for a moment. He had to be very careful to get the jeep away from the edge. He climbed out of the passenger side. As soon as he put his feet down on the ice, they flew out from under him and he landed on his rear end. Cursing, he spat blood from a split lip. He rose gingerly and, holding on to the jeep, inched his way back to the door and climbed inside. He buckled his seat belt and then started the engine. It coughed and sputtered, but soon the steady hum of the motor assured him he was ready to go. He shifted into drive and eased his foot off the brake and onto the gas pedal. The jeep began to slide immediately. He panicked and slammed on the brakes, but the left front wheel had already slipped over the edge. The jeep teetered and then tilted sideways off the ledge. It began to slide, first slowly and then faster, breaking branches and downing sapling pines. It halted against a dead birch. Snow fell like a blizzard shrouding the inside of the vehicle in total darkness.

He was safe. Then he heard a crunch as the dead wood gave away, the jeep began tumbling down the deep scree. He screamed as he flung his hands about, futilely searching for a way to brace himself. Kyle's watch spun off and hit the dash. The jeep ricocheted and rebounded down more than 150 feet and exploded into a fireball.

Kyle's *Rolex,* tossed to the side at the bottom of the ravine, faithfully recorded the man's death at 11.03 A.M.

CHAPTER 25

———◆———

GARETH MORTON STUDIED A TOPOGRAPHICAL map of Maine he had spread out on his kitchen table. He scrutinized the Bangor area and then picked up the copy of the ransom-note Richard Sloan had given him. It consisted of letters laboriously glued in from magazines and other printed material in an unwieldly format. The postmark indicated Madison, ME. He estimated the distance between Bangor and Madison at about 30 miles. He flung his pencil across the map. *Where are you, you creep?*

He crossed the floor, opened the refrigerator, and reached for a beer.

"Why don't you come to bed, honey?" Lindsay, his wife stood in the doorway. She stretched and yawned. "It's ten o'clock."

"Yes, I know, but I can't sleep. This case is bugging me. This guy's location is critical. I've gotta find where the scumbag is keeping Kyle, time is of the essence. There are so many things working against a successful search and rescue, with the weather being on top of the list."

Gareth gave her a hug and led her back to the bedroom. "You get some sleep, sweetheart, you've got to go to work tomorrow." He kissed her and pulled the covers on top of her. "I'll be in shortly," he said and left the room.

Back in the kitchen, he squinted at the map. His eyes roamed the area around Madison. *Where could he be?*

The phone rang, and he quickly answered.

"Gareth, Richard Sloan here. Sorry about the late call, but I've got some news."

"Shoot."

"A police helicopter spotted a burning vehicle."

"So?"

"Well, it's the location that's kind of suspicious."

"What do you mean?"

"As far as they could tell from air, the vehicle went over a steep slope in a mountainous, isolated area in Western Maine. Mt. Blue. There was a blizzard the night before, and access to the area is not possible for several days."

"I don't see a connection here, Mr. Sloan."

"Frankly, I don't either. Let's just say I have a gut feeling. I've asked the police to keep me informed on anything happening out of the ordinary, and this incident falls into the category."

Gareth, his foot on one of the kitchen chairs, chewed on his lower lip for a moment and then straightened up.

"Gareth, are you there…"

"Yes, Mr. Sloan. I have to go up there to see for myself."

"All right. Keep me posted." Richard Sloan hung up.

Gareth turned out the light as he left the kitchen. In the bedroom, he undressed quickly, jumped into bed, and snuggled up to his wife who snored softly. He closed his eyes and fell into a deep sleep.

The following morning after breakfast, Gareth kissed his wife and told her he'd be gone for a few days, jumped in his truck, and headed for Mt. Blue. Road crews had made some progress, and he encountered no trouble driving until he reached the park. There he followed the snow covered road that snaked through the pine forest. The elevation increased steadily as he approached several police vehicles and two state forest SUV's. He parked the old Ford and got out of the vehicle. A man wearing a hooded ski jacket strode toward him.

Waving a badge in Gareth's face, he yelled, "Sir, this is a crime scene. Please turn around and leave immediately."

"I know. That's why I'm here." Gareth whipped out his business card and handed it to the officer. "I'm investigating the case."

The man scrutinized the card and pocketed it. "I think I better hold on to this, just in case."

"Help yourself," Gareth said impatiently and walked toward the stretcher covered with a tarp. The officer followed.

"Any ID?" Gareth lifted a corner of the tarp and shrank back. He turned his head and let out a breath. The charred remains in front of him bore no resemblance to a human being. He dropped the tarp and stepped back as the medics deposited the stretcher into the ambulance.

"Any idea who this is?"

"No. Burned beyond recognition. Not much left of his vehicle either." The officer shook his head. "What fool would navigate these roads during a blizzard?"

"A criminal."

"Well, at this point, we're still investigating. We did find this." He removed a plastic bag from his pocket containing a battered but working watch with pieces of an expendable metal band still attached. "It's a *Rolex*," the officer volunteered unnecessarily.

"May I?" Gareth reached for it and the officer reluctantly dropped it into his hand. Gareth studied the watch carefully. It was a *Rolex* all right. *Probably stolen.* He turned it over. The steel plate in back was covered with soot. He took out his handkerchief and wiped it. The description came up: To Kyle from Amy. He gave it to the agent whose eyebrows shot up.

"Do you think these are the remains of Kyle Weldon?"

"Don't know," the police officer returned the watch into the plastic bag. "We'll find out soon enough."

"Hello."

"Gareth Morton. I've got some interesting news."

"Where are you?"

"Sheffield. Small borough near Mt. Blue."

"Shoot," Richard Sloan said.

"I was at the crash scene. They discovered one charred body. Impossible to tell if the remains are those of a woman or a man. The police officer I spoke with is certain that positive identification will be made through dental records…"

"But they have no clue who this could be," Richard interrupted irritably.

"Oh, but they do, at least one clue. They recovered a watch. An expensive watch with an inscription reading To Kyle from Amy."

Richard's stomach clenched, and he said slowly, "This must be Kyle. Amy is my daughter. They had a relationship." He paused, and remained silent. His mind raced in turmoil. Kyle, dead. Burned to a crisp while having a murder charge hanging over him. *I know he didn't kill that woman. He couldn't have. I'm a pretty good judge of character, and something here does not make sense.*

"It's a *Rolex*," Gareth said.

Richard sighed heavily, "Yes, that would be the kind of present my daughter gives to…" His voice broke, and his shoulders dropped.

"Mr. Sloan, I'm not convinced that this is Kyle's body. Let's just say I have a hunch. I will stay here for a day or so and do some investigating if that's okay with you."

Richard's head shot up, and he said quickly, "Do whatever you think necessary. I want you to get to the bottom of this tragedy. I owe this boy after what my daughter has done to him." Static in the phone line clouded his last words.

"Pardon, I couldn't hear the last part," Gareth said with raised voice.

"Never mind. Do your job and keep me posted."

"Yes, Sir." Gareth hung up.

CHAPTER 26

KYLE PEERED THROUGH THE CRACK in the door. Strips of sunshine pierced through the opening, blinding him temporarily. A heavy blanket of snow from the blizzard covered the area as far as he could see. There was no sign of tire tracks. The silence that lingered for at least two days now unnerved him and he no longer could dismiss his fear. He turned and fed the stove. He kept the fire low, for he was running out of wood. His food supply consisted of one slice of bread, a smidgeon of peanut butter, and a half empty bottle of water.

The bucket in the corner, filled to the brim, released a steady stench. He walked to the door. "Hey, you son-of-a-bitch," he hollered as loud as he could, "open the door."

A light breeze brushed against the pine trees dropping clumps of snow. "Hey," he cried, hammering the door with both fists. "I need wood, I need food. You can't leave me out here to die." There was no sign of anyone. This was it, starve or freeze to death—whatever came first. For the umpteenth time, he scanned the walls and ceiling for any possibility of escape. The little shed was solid. Besides, he had no tools. He was doomed. His head fell against his chest and panic flooded his mind. *Mustn't lose control. Got to find a way out of here.* He crossed over to the cot and dropped onto it. With his legs drawn up closely, he wrapped the blanket tightly around him and rested his back against the wall. The eerie glow of the dying fire spread a ghostly display across the ceiling. A steady stream of cold air crept into the shed.

Gareth checked into a small hotel. In his room, he took off his coat and dropped onto the bed. He didn't make much progress today. *Where are you, Kyle? Why do I have this weird feeling you're still alive?* He rose abruptly. He ran his fingers through his hair and down his face. He needed a shave. He walked over to the mirror. Lindsay would be on his case if she saw him right now. He looked at the empty bed. He missed her. He never slept well when he worked out of town on a case. He reached for his cell phone.

"Hello."

"Hi, sweetheart."

"Hey, where are you?"

"Some dinky town in Maine...actually it's a very nice little town," he said.

"I miss you."

"Yeah, me too, babe."

"When are you coming home?"

"In a day or two. I've got some exploring to do."

On the other end of the line, Lindsay nodded. He never liked to talk about a case. She respected his work ethics. Though her curiosity sometimes got the better of her, she learned to manage it.

"Is it snowing up there?" she asked.

"Not now. There's lots of snow on the ground." He kicked off his shoes and yawned. "I guess I better get some sleep. I've got a long day tomorrow."

"Be careful. Promise me."

"I'm always careful. Love you, Babe," he said and hung up. His spirit rallied as he made his plans. He must go up that mountain.

The next morning Gareth left the small hotel and skipped down the steps. He pulled up his collar as he headed toward the crowded eatery across the street. He needed a strong cup of coffee. He rubbed his hands. It was bitter cold, and he had left his gloves at home. Making a mental note to drop in at the country store next to the eatery, he shoved his hands deeply into the pockets of his down-filled jacket.

The sound of three bells attached to the top of the door announced his arrival at the eatery. The small room was lined with booths filled with customers, but two empty chairs faced the counter. Sitting down, he looked up at the clock on the wall: Twelve noon. A middle aged woman wearing a red and white checkered apron approached him and followed his gaze. She giggled and said, "One of these days I'll get that clock fixed." She wiped the area in front of Gareth with a clean rag and added, "We don't care much about time 'round here." She looked him straight in the eyes, "What'll it be."

Gareth smiled. He liked her. "Coffee, strong, two eggs over light, and three strips of bacon."

"Coming right up."

He glanced around the room. He judged most of the clients to be seniors of varying vintage. They looked relaxed and comfortable having breakfast with family or friends.

"You must be new in town. I'm Gwen" The woman offered her hand.

"Gareth Morton." He gripped hers firmly.

She served the coffee and within a few minutes returned with a steaming plate of food. The aroma tickled Gareth's nostrils and he realized he was ravenous. He began to eat with gusto. Gwen stood and watched. "Delicious," Gareth said chewing heartily.

She grinned. "We aim to please." She turned and picked up the coffee carafe and refilled his cup.

Gareth wiped his mouth. He leaned back and sighed with pleasure. Gwen approached. "Anything else?"

"No, thanks. I'm stuffed. My compliments to the chef for a truly outstanding breakfast."

"That'll be my husband Owen. I'll let him know." She turned to leave.

"Wait a minute, Gwen. I want to ask you a question."

She scrunched her forehead. "I thought so," she mumbled. Out loud she said. "Shoot. Are you some kind of detective?"

Gareth let out a burst of laughter. "As a matter of fact I am. How did you know?"

Her face softened. "You've got that look about you."

Gareth raised his eyebrows. "What look?"

"Oh, I don't know. I guess I'm clairvoyant." She leaned on the counter and brought her face close to his. "What do you want to know?"

"I'm sure you've heard there's been an accident on Mt. Blue…"

"Oh yes, the crash. Only a fool would drive up there in this kind of weather."

"Does anyone live there?"

"No, but there are isolated cabins hunters use. They're empty. Hunting season is over." She looked at him suspiciously and straightened up. "You'd better tell me what you're after."

Gareth grinned and said. "Have you seen any strangers in your restaurant lately?"

"No."

"A woman was murdered in Port Clyde, and the suspect has disappeared." He pulled a photo of Kyle out of his pocket given to him by Richard Sloan.

Gwen examined it closely. She shook her head. "Never seen this guy."

"Are you sure?"

"Absolutely." She studied the photo. "He has a nice, gentle face," she said. "He doesn't look like a murderer."

"I don't think he did it, but he has disappeared, and that makes him a prime suspect."

"Gwen," a voice called from the kitchen.

"Here is my card," Gareth said. "Call me if he shows up, will you?"

"You can count on it. Good luck, I hope you find him." She nodded and rushed off. Gareth finished his coffee, threw money on the counter and left.

The door boasted a sign "Get everything cheap HERE!" Gareth chuckled and entered the store. He looked around. Incredible! The cramped shelves held toilet plungers, soup cans, hammers, chain saws, pillows—even feminine pads. He got a shopping cart and went through the aisles. Twenty minutes later, he paid for his purchases and left the store. He was pleased. He had found everything he needed: gloves, a back pack, several bottles of water, granola bars, and three flares. The golden arches sign across the street caught his attention. He'd need some food on his trek up Mt. Blue. He entered McDonalds and bought a couple hamburgers and fries. He got into his truck, stuffed his purchases into the back pack, tossed it onto the rear seat, and started the engine.

He stopped at the Sheffield Police Department, a squat brick structure which may have been a bank forty years ago. Presenting his business card to the clerk, he said, "I'm investigating the Kyle Weldon case. I'd like to speak to someone..."

"That would be me." A muscular man with a bald head and friendly face came through the doorway and extended his hand. "Sergeant Bilko."

Gareth smiled at him widely, and Bilko said, "No comments please, I've heard it all."

Gareth shook his hand. "Gareth Morton, and I had no intention of making a comment. I'm investigating the Kyle Weldon case."

"All I can tell you is we still don't know the identity of the crash victim, although based on dental records, we know for certain it's not Kyle Weldon," Bilko said.

"I'd like to go up on the mountain and investigate the crash site and the area in general. I'd like to see for myself..."

"Go right ahead. We're still searching for any clues. As soon as the weather breaks, we'll get the helicopter up there. They've already made one search. All they saw was a pack of wolves rummaging through the debris."

"Wolves?"

"Yes, so if you're going up there be forewarned. My advice to you is be damned careful!"

The phone trilled. "Sergeant, it's for you."

"Excuse me," Bilko said and brushed by Gareth. He listened for a minute and then cupped the mouthpiece and said, "This will take a while. Was there anything else?"

"No, thanks for your time." Gareth saluted the sergeant, and then added, "I've got a couple flares. Just in case I stumble upon anything."

Bilko rolled his eyes. "All right. Hopefully, we'll be able to get the chopper up there later today." He turned his back to Gareth.

CHAPTER 27

—◆—

LUKE SAT ON THE PORCH swing with Peggy. She bore a striking resemblance to Lisa. When he spotted her on the college campus, he began pursuing her tirelessly. Even after she admitted she was seeing someone else, he convinced her to go out with him.

He reached for her hand, squeezed it, leaned closer and nuzzled her ear. A car turned into the driveway. Luke dropped Peggy's hand, and he straightened up. Lisa got out of the car and hurried toward the porch. Looking straight ahead, she climbed the steps and rang the doorbell.

"Hello there," Luke said.

Startled, Lisa turned her head. "Luke, I didn't see you. I…" She spotted the girl.

"Meet my friend Peggy," Luke said quickly.

"Hi Peggy." Lisa waved just as Joan opened the door.

"Come in."

Lisa disappeared inside. Luke stared after her. He had staged the whole thing. He knew she was coming and had rushed to get Peggy to be there when Lisa arrived. His head dropped as he wondered what she would say when she found out Kyle may be dead. Would she turn to him? Beg him to comfort her? Well, she missed her chance. He put his arm around Peggy and drew her close.

"That's all I know," Joan said after she finished telling Lisa about the accident and the watch.

"Tell me again what the inscription said?"

"To Kyle from Amy."

"Amy."

"Yes," Joan said. "Amy was the woman he was involved with in Portland."

Lisa jumped up with such force the chair fell back. She ignored it and paced the kitchen floor. "That doesn't mean Kyle is dead. I simply don't believe it." She brought her hand up to her forehead.

"They will know for sure shortly through his dental records. I've told the police the name of our dentist. I expect to hear from them soon."

"I'm furious with the papers. Calling him a murder suspect. What's his motive? He's no criminal. Anyone who's ever met Kyle knows this."

Joan pointed to a chair. "Come, sit down. I'll make us a cup of tea. We'll know the truth soon. Until then, we'll have to be strong."

"I know, but this waiting makes me crazy. Suppose he's hurt, and there's no one to help him…"

"I know. All we can do is pray. The rest is up to the police. They'll get to the bottom of this. How do you think I feel? After I lost my husband, my whole world collapsed. It was the boys who kept me going." She reached across the table and took Lisa's hand. "I can't even imagine losing Kyle." She squeezed Lisa's hand forcefully until Lisa winced. Joan let go and rose to attend the whistling tea kettle.

"I pray for him every day, although I must admit, it doesn't give me much comfort." Joan sighed and dropped teabags into two mugs.

Dusk had descended across the yard when Lisa stepped out the front door and turned to Joan. The two women hugged. "Bye, Lisa," Joan said. "I'll keep you posted, I promise."

Lisa nodded mutely and walked away, her shoulders hunched, her mouth quivering. She didn't look at Luke and Peggy. Luke felt a moment's jealousy, recognized it for what it was, and dismissed it. "So long, Lisa" he said softly.

When Lisa arrived at Acadia Avenue, the screen door opened and a little boy dashed down the porch steps just as she parked the car in the driveway.

"Andy, wait." Lisa's mother ran after him.

"Mommy!"

Lisa closed her eyes for a second. How she wished she were his mommy. Hopefully the adoption would go through. In the meantime, she had custody and he was living with her in her parents' house. She got out of the car and stretched out her arms.

"Andy!" she called. She picked him up and swung him up into the air, and he squealed with delight. When she wanted to put him down he held on tightly and pressed his face against hers. "I love you," he whispered.

A lump rose in Lisa's throat and she hugged him to her. "Mommy loves you too."

"Are you going to stay out there all evening? Supper is ready," her mom said.

"Coming." Lisa put Andy down, took his hand, and together they ran up the steps.

"Let's say prayers." They sat around the dinner table. "Andy, it's your turn," Lisa's father said.

"Okay." The little boy's face grew serious. He folded his hands and said, "Dear God, bless the macaroni and cheese. It's my favorite," and then he added, "and bless the fried chicken too."

"Amen."

CHAPTER 28

———◆———

KYLE TURNED TO HIS SIDE. Daylight. In spite of his hunger and thirst, he'd slept all night. If only he weren't so cold. He tried to pull the blanket tighter around him, but his hand dropped. He didn't have the energy. He shivered and closed his eyes. *Am I dying? Is this how it is?* Pictures of his mom and dad and Luke passed through his mind, like a slow-moving video. They were hiking the Grand Canyon. His father explained the eons of rock formation to the boys. Kyle could hear his words as clearly as if he stood next to him. "Nearly two billion years of Earth's geological history have been exposed as the Colorado River and its tributaries cut their channels through layer after layer of rock while the Colorado Plateau was uplifted. Think about it; scientists know now that the Colorado River established its course through the canyon at least 17 million years ago."

The image of his dad faded, and Kyle shifted, unable to get comfortable. *I always wanted to go back there some day. Now I wonder if I'll get the chance.* He looked around his dismal prison. *Is this it? Am I going to die here? Dad, you always knew what to do. Please help me.* He remembered his father had a strong faith in God that had sustained him during the war. He often mentioned it in his letters. *Pray for me* used to be his closing words, and they did. Every day, before they had their dinner, Joan would lead them in prayer asking God to keep Gregg safe. *Pray.* The word rang in his ears. His head rolled from side to side. *Pray.* He opened his eyes. *God, please help me.* He mouthed the words. Tears rolled down his cheeks, and he licked them from his chapped lips. His mouth was dry and his throat ached. He coughed and then lay still.

"Mrs. Weldon, Richard Sloan here."

Joan's hand began to shake as she held the receiver. "Mr. Sloan..."

"I have good news. The Portland police informed me the dental records of the victim do not match Kyle's."

"Thank God! But whose are they?" she said and then the impact of his statement hit her. "Oh Mr. Sloan, that means Kyle is still alive, doesn't it?" Before he could reply she added, "And he *is* innocent."

"Yes, Mrs. Weldon, I know he's innocent."

"But where could Kyle be?"

"They're looking for him, and so is the private investigator I engaged. Don't worry, Mrs. Weldon, we'll find Kyle," he assured her.

She nodded. The news was good, but she found she was still confused and apprehensive.

He read her thoughts. "I know you're still worried. And rightfully so. I believe there is hope we'll find Kyle...alive. And you must believe it too."

"Yes, I know. Thank you, Mr. Sloan. Please let me know as soon as you hear anything."

"Of course. Good bye, Mrs. Weldon."

"Bye." She hung up. Her forehead creased, and she bit her lip. She wanted to scream, smash something, kick the door. What more was expected of her? First Gregg and now Kyle. The doorbell rang, *Go away. I don't want to see anyone.* She rose wearily and headed for the stairs. The ringing continued, and then someone banged on the door.

"Joan, open up. It's Vince."

She hesitated, then turned and walked slowly toward the door. She opened it and he entered. He took one look at her and stepped forward and drew her into his arms. She began to cry and buried her face against his chest. He held her close. When he finally released her, he pushed the door shut and led her into the living room. They sat, and he took her hand into his. "Richard Sloan called me. He was worried about you."

She leaned against him. "I'm glad you came. I'm in pretty bad shape."

"I can see that. Let me fix you a cup of tea. Have you had breakfast?"

"A cup of tea will be fine. I don't want anything to eat."

"Coming up." He took her shoes off and made her lie down on the sofa. He removed the throw from the rocking chair and covered her. He kissed her on the forehead. "I'll be right back."

Joan closed her eyes. When he returned with the tea, she was fast asleep. He sat next to her. "Don't worry," he murmured. "I'll be right here when you wake up."

Gareth parked the truck about a mile below the crash scene. This was as far as he was able to drive. The snow-choked trail snaked up the mountain. He checked his watch: 10.05 A.M., and he began the hike. About an hour later, he spotted the topped-off trees. He stood at the ridge and stared down at the burnt, soot-covered spot where the jeep had landed. He surveyed the snowpack around him. The toppled trees showed the direction the jeep had been coming. He determined the only way to go was up, so he headed that way. As he ploughed forward the forest became less dense. He raised his binoculars and scanned the perimeter. Nothing. Just clumps of trees and lots of snow all the way around. He uttered a curse and trudged forward and upward.

The clouds thinned allowing tepid sunshine to dapple the snow. He stopped at a rock, wiped off clumps of ice, and sat down. He had made only modest progress and already his legs ached. He vowed to hit the gym once he got back. Lindsay had tried to get him to go with her, but he declined. His job provided him with enough exercise and footwork, what did he need a gym for?

"Look at your belly, honey," Lindsay had teased. "You used to be a size 32 waist and now…" Before she could finish, he'd thrown a pillow at her, and she retaliated. He got up and chased her and they had ended up in bed. Afterward Gareth said, "Sex is the best exercise there is." He had turned to his wife, who was already asleep, her lips turned up into a soft smile.

Gareth smiled as he thought of his wife and began to eat his hamburger and soggy fries. Chewing on the cold food he looked around. It had taken him over two hours to get this far. Calculating the time he needed to get back to his vehicle before dark, he didn't have much time left. "Damn." He crunched the hamburger wrapper and flung it into the air. It landed in the snow not far from him. He stared at it for a minute, then rose wearily, picked it up and shoved it into his pocket. He put his gloves back on and continued the hike, his boots crunching through the frozen snow and ice frustrating his upward progress.

CHAPTER 29

———

GARETH BROUGHT THE BINOCULARS UP to his eyes and searched the area. The pine trees had shed most of the snow, but low-growing vegetation was still covered. Should he turn back or continue the search? His watch showed 1:30 P.M. He looked at the sky. The clouds made way for bright sunshine and he decided to move on. He noticed he had naturally gravitated to what might be a path or an animal trail or even a roadbed. When he tried to kick at the snow and ice to get a glimpse of what was underneath, he spotted what could have been tire tracks. Encouraged, he trudged forward. Other than the slight breeze whispering in the tree tops, a disquieting silence dominated the mountain.

His breath came in quick puffs. He gave up smoking twenty years ago when his best friend, Todd, was diagnosed with lung cancer. The experience had scared the crap out of him. No one got cancer at 24, or so he thought. Witnessing the chemo and its consequences the loss of hair, the vomiting, and the rash inside Todd's mouth and throat had convinced Gareth to never to touch a cigarette again. Todd survived but barely.

Gareth paused when he heard the howl. It broke the spell of the silence, and he strained to listen. Nothing. He released his breath and kept on walking. There it was again. He halted his step and scanned the region with the binoculars. He knew there were wolves all over the Northern American continent. Their cries could be heard up to 70 miles away. The high pitched howls were distinct and he hoped the wolves roamed somewhere in the far distance. His hand involuntary reached for his Smith and Wesson 38 revolver tucked inside the holster attached to his belt. He pulled it out and checked the cylinder. It was fully loaded. He pushed it inside the holster and leaned against the tree. Beads of perspiration clustered on his forehead. Maybe it would be smart to go back while he was still able. He didn't scare easy, but the thought of battling wolves created some alarm.

The odd sensation in his gut, however, would not leave him alone; he felt he was close to something. Maybe it was wishful thinking. He had no proof of Kyle being anywhere near here. He squatted and pulled out a chocolate bar. He chewed slowly savoring the sweetness, grateful for having purchased several at the last minute. Suddenly, he realized he was looking at something incongruous: tire tracks leading westward. On his knees, he crawled forward and carefully moved some of the frozen snow. He exposed enough tracking to confirm that a vehicle had passed here some time ago. He jumped up, pocketed his chocolate bar wrapper, and pushed forward with renewed energy.

God, please let me find this boy. I'll do anything you want. I'll even take the neighbor's bratty kids to the ball game as Lindsay had suggested so many times, but only let me find Kyle.

By late afternoon he paused and checked his watch: 4:30 P.M. Raising the binoculars he searched the range. He cursed and let them drop to his chest. No sign of life anywhere. Even the birds were silent. He looked down and studied the ground covered with isolated patches of frozen snow. He dropped to one knee, and brushed his hand across the hard surface. Any evidence of tire tracks had disappeared. Maybe he should turn back; after all, he didn't want to get stuck in the woods for the night with wolves roaming the area. His hand reached to his side, and patted the holster holding the revolver. He got up and stood for a moment. What to do? His instincts were pushing him forward, yet he couldn't ignore the danger. He glanced at his watch again. It would be dark in less than two hours. He could still make it back to his vehicle. He inhaled deeply and continued to walk ahead.

A short time later, he paused for a drink of water. He raised the bottle to his mouth, closed his eyes and drank deeply. He fastened the cap and stood still, his hands on his hips. In front of him stood a young pine tree with several of its branches snapped. Some had fallen to the ground. He picked up one of the branches and then looked up. His heart beat faster as he squinted and reached for his binoculars. About 500 feet in front of him, the snow-covered beams of a structure peaked through a cluster of low-growing holly trees.

He tried to run, fell, rose and finally reached the low front porch of a small, crude log cabin. He stepped onto the porch and tried the door. It was unlocked. He entered the dark interior. Once his eyes adjusted, he studied his surroundings. The one window gave little light, but he stood in what must be the living and sleeping area. Farther to the right stood a woodstove, its exhaust pipe reaching up and through the ceiling. Soot and grime covered the entire wall, including the cabinet hanging lopsided, its doors open and revealing a few pots and plates. Cigarette butts in a coffee cup on the table, and a blanket scattered on the dirty sofa indicated someone had been here lately. Was it the creep he was looking for? Some accomplice? But where was Kyle? He stepped outside and walked around the structure and saw the shed. As soon as he spotted the padlock on the door, his stomach tightened into a knot. He yanked on the chain. No use. He pulled out his revolver and blasted the lock. He flung the door back and the diminishing light of day crept inside. He turned his head when the stench hit him. He rushed inside and discovered the body on the cot.

CHAPTER 30

———◆———

GARETH PLACED HIS HAND ON Kyle's cold forehead and then fell to his knees, put his head onto his chest and listened. He could not detect a heartbeat, and immediately began CPR. *Come on, Kyle. Wake up.* He worked feverishly. His body heat rose and the heavy outer wear became like a furnace. He was panting. *Can't stop.* Again, his head dropped onto Kyle's chest. There it was, a faint heartbeat. He moved his face close to Kyle's nose and felt the breath. Kyle opened his eyes which widened with fear

"Don't worry, you're safe. Gareth Morton. I'm an investigator."

Kyle shivered. "Cold," he mouthed the words.

Gareth removed his heavy jacket and draped it around Kyle. Then he pulled the filthy blanket up and covered him up to his neck. The boy was suffering from severe hypothermia. Gareth had to bring his temperature up.

Suddenly, a putrid smell hit his nostrils, and he recoiled. He looked around and discovered the overflowing bucket. He picked it up with both hands, hurried outside, dumped its contents into the bushes, and then dropped it when he saw the pile of wood adjacent to the shed. He picked up as much as he could carry, and on the way back inside, he wondered about matches. No longer a smoker, he had thrown his lighter in the trash on the first smokeless day many years ago.

"Water," Kyle whispered.

"Yes, of course." Gareth dug in his backpack and pulled out a bottle of water. He lifted Kyle's head and brought the bottle to his mouth. Kyle gulped.

"Slow, take it slow," Gareth cautioned.

Kyle blinked and stopped. His hand reached for the bottle. Gareth hesitated. "Take it slow."

"I will."

A shiver shot through Gareth's body. He needed to get the fire started. When a search for matches in the shed proved unsuccessful, he headed to the cabin. He rummaged in the kitchen area and found a box of matches on the table next to a dented kettle. He gathered both items, hurried back to the shed and started the fire.

"I'll close the door in a minute, Kyle. We need some fresh air in here. How are you feeling?"

"I'm hungry and cold. I have never been so cold in my life. I thought I was going to die for sure."

"Well, you're not dead. We need to get this place warmed up. I saw some peanut butter in the cabin. I'm going to get it. Maybe there's some other foodstuff, and then you can tell me what happened if you feel up to it."

A reddish glow emanating from the stove spread welcome warmth. Gareth went outside to fill the kettle with snow. On his way he retrieved the bucket. Darkness had descended on the mountain. He placed the kettle on the stove. Maybe there's some tea or coffee at the cabin. Lots of warm liquid was needed here. It looked like the boy was rallying, and he must get him to eat. They would have to spend the night on the mountain for sure. Tomorrow he'll think of a way to get back to civilization.

Walking over to the cabin, he checked his cell phone; it was dead. He spat a curse as he stepped through the open door. After a brief search he discovered two jars of peanut butter, a steak knife, and empty candy bar wrapper. Ah, that was a reminder; he still had several chocolate bars in his back pack. There was no sign of coffee or tea but he found a cup with a broken handle. On his way out he spotted a flashlight hanging on the inside of the door next to a faded, worn tote bag. He put everything but the flashlight inside the tote and stepped outside.

He turned on the flashlight and saw the wolf, standing close to the bushes not far from where Gareth had emptied the bucket. Fragments of snow glittered on his gray mottled fur. His eyes blazed, and he began to snarl. Gareth stood still keeping the light beam on the wolf. He recalled having read wolves infected with rabies usually travel alone. They developed the disease to a very high degree making rabid wolves perhaps the most dangerous of all rabid animals. A quick glance around assured him the wolf was alone. He knew the next minute or two could decide his life or death, so he must act smartly. He dug deep in his brain for all he knew about how to avoid triggering an attack. He evaded eye contact with the beast, lowered his head, and bowed slightly, as he stepped sideways, slowly, until he reached the shed. The wolf growled and just as he began lunging toward him, Gareth dashed inside and slammed the door shut. He leaned against the rough wood and released the breath he'd been holding. He dropped the tote, and pointed the flashlight at Kyle, who rested on the cot, his eyes closed.

Gareth directed the light beam around the interior of the shed. He needed to secure the door. It looked like the cot was the only suitable barricade.

"Kyle," he called out.

The door rattled, and he could hear snarls and scratching. Gareth planted his feet firmly into the ground and pressed his back hard against the door. "Kyle, wake up."

Kyle stirred and raised his head.

"I need your help. We must secure this door."

Kyle tried to get to his feet, when he brought his hand to his eyes, and dropped back on the cot. "I'm dizzy, Gareth," he said.

"Kyle, can you reach inside my backpack, right there next to the cot. I've got some candy bars inside." Kyle leaned over and grabbed the bag. He located the candy bar, tore the wrapper and devoured it.

Gareth noted the silence. The commotion outside had stopped. Maybe the wolf had given up. Hopefully, he didn't leave to gather his relatives. Gareth looked at Kyle. "How about helping me here? Can you do it?"

"I'll try. I heard the wolf howling and scratching the door yesterday." He rose shakily and staggered toward Gareth.

"Lean against the door until I move the cot over." Gareth tried to pull the cot away from the wall. It was heavier than he thought. *I guess that's a good thing.* He strained and pulled, and inch by inch he managed to drag it in front the door. He sat down and wiped the perspiration from his forehead. "Sit," he said to Kyle. "We'll be spending the night on this thing."

Kyle dropped down next to him. The water on the stove had reached the boiling point, and Gareth poured some into the cup. "Here," he said, "drink this. We've got to get your body temperature up."

Kyle drank from the cup, swallowing slowly, until it was empty. He handed it back to Gareth. "Do you have any more candy bars?" He asked.

Gareth shook his head. "How about some peanut butter instead?"

Kyle managed a crooked grin. "Okay… but if I ever get out of here, I'll never touch that stuff again as long as I live."

Gareth patted him on the back and laughed. "Here…" he handed Kyle the jar of peanut butter and the steak knife. "I couldn't locate any spoons. Just be careful and don't cut your tongue." He reached for the kettle and poured another cup of warm water. He leaned back and watched Kyle eat.

When Kyle was finished, he gave Gareth the knife and the jar. "Want to try some?"

"Don't mind if I do." Gareth dipped the knife inside and took a mouthful. He frowned. "I like the crunchy kind better." They both chuckled. Then Gareth got serious and said, "How about telling me what happened to you? From the beginning, starting at Marshall Point after you discovered Melanie's body. And you *did* discover her body, didn't you?" Gareth rose and fed the stove. He turned to Kyle, "How about it?"

Kyle nodded and began to tell his story.

"That's all of it," he said when he was finished. "You can dissect it and make some sense out of it, but if you don't mind, I'm going to sleep." He drew up his legs, rested his head on his knees and closed his eyes.

Gareth regarded him sympathetically. He liked the kid. What an experience! He'd been through a lot. He purposely didn't tell Kyle about the murder warrant. No need to worry him with it now. Everything would be straightened out once they got back to the police station. Gareth stared at the red hot stove. They had enough wood until morning. *Tomorrow is going to be interesting. Hopefully wolf will be gone. Or maybe he'll be back with his family. No matter, I'll be ready for them. I have every intention of getting out of here alive.* He checked his revolver again; the cylinder was fully loaded.

CHAPTER 31

———◆———

SERGEANT BILKO PUSHED HIS CHAIR back. The schoolhouse clock on the wall struck 9:00 P.M. He frowned. Time to go home. He'd be in trouble again. He'd missed dinner three times in a row this week. His face softened, and he silently vowed to make it up to her. Emily, his wife, knew what his job demanded, but she had her limits. This evening, he hung around the station doing paperwork in hopes of catching that PI from Portland who drove up the mountain this morning. Maybe his trip was fruitless, and he had returned and checked into his room already in order to get some sleep.

He reached for his hat and walked out the door. He stopped at the front desk.

"Hey, Jake, did that detective show up by any chance?"

"Gareth Morton? No I haven't seen him since I came on duty at 6:00 P.M."

"Morton, yeah, that's his name. Listen, if you hear from him, have him call me at home. He has my card."

"Sure thing, Sarge," Jake said and gave a sloppy salute.

"Thanks. See you in the morning." Bilko walked outside, pulling his collar up against the cold. He looked at the clear night sky. Stars glittered like diamonds. He shivered. The freezing temperatures had arrived early this year, winter hadn't even officially begun. He made a mental note to check on Morton in the morning if he didn't hear from him tonight. He got into his car and left the parking lot.

———◆———

Gareth stirred. He didn't get much sleep. He sat up and rotated his neck. His whole body ached, and he shivered. The temperatures must be close to freezing inside the shed. The fire had died sometime in the wee hours. *Damn.* He slipped into his jacket, cleaned out the ashes, piling them in the corner of the shed, and started a new fire. He walked back to the cot. Kyle was still asleep. A quick glance at his watch: 7:10 A.M. Fingers of light began to invade the shed. He pressed the side of his face against the crack in the door. The wind chattered as it swept frozen leaves into a frenzy. No sign of the wolf as far as he could tell.

Kyle stirred and stretched, yawning loudly. "Morning. See anything out there?"

"No. There's a full cloud cover. Looks like we're going to get more snow." He reached for the backpack and pulled out the last water bottle. "Here," he said, handing it to Kyle. He reached for the jar of peanut butter. "That is the last of the peanut butter." They ate until the knife scraped the bottom. "Well, now we're out of food, but it doesn't matter," Gareth said, "we're leaving this hellhole today."

They took turns drinking from the water bottle, when Kyle coughed and cleared his throat. "I want to thank you…for saving my life," he said. "I thought my time had come. I knew I was going to die, right here in this stinking shed, with the wolves tearing at the door. And then you arrived. I owe you my life."

"I'm glad I got here in time. How are you feeling?"

"Weak and a little dizzy."

"We need to get you to a hospital for sure."

Sergeant Bilko entered the police station. He spent a restless night and was in a bad mood. He kept waiting for the phone to ring. Somehow, he could not get Morton out of his mind. He must find out what happened. They didn't need another needless death in the little community of Sheffield.

"Any news of Morton?" he barked. The officer at the desk jumped up and frantically searched the papers on the desk.

"Answer me!"

"No Sarge. There is no message from the night clerk and since I've come on duty, the phone hasn't rung once."

"Let's get the chopper ready. I want that mountain searched. They should spot the detective's truck. The damn fool. We've gotta find him before he freezes to death or the wolves get him." Bilko stomped into his office and threw his coat onto a chair.

———◆———

The police helicopter circled the area. A heavy cloud cover hung across the sky, and light snow filled the air. The pilot squinted as he searched the ground. Poor visibility prevented him from spotting the smoke rising through the chimney in the shed below.

Gareth raised his head at that moment and Kyle exclaimed, "I hear something."

They strained to listen. "It's a chopper," Gareth said and searched for the flare in the backpack. He pulled out his revolver and jumped up.

"What're you going to do?"

"I'll signal them. Come, let's get this cot out of the way."

Kyle was already on his feet, and together they pulled the wobbly cot away from the door. Gareth opened the door ajar and directed one eye outside. He could hear the helicopter engine as did the wolf, which had retreated to the edge of the brush, his eyes focused on the shed. Gareth raised the revolver just as the wolf got to his feet ready to attack. The shot rattled the shed, and the wolf yelped and dropped to the ground. Taking cautious steps, Gareth left the shed. The dead wolf lay in a puddle of blood. Gareth shot the flare into the sky. The snow fell more heavily, and the sky was cloaked in clouds. He doubted the pilot could spot the signal.

"Let's go," he said to Kyle who was standing above the dead wolf.

"I wish I had my camera."

Gareth let out a snort. "We've got to get out of here. Can you make it?" Before Kyle could answer, Gareth added, "We've got no choice." He pointed to the wolf. "I'm afraid his relatives will show up shortly. This is our only chance to get away."

"I'm fine. Don't worry about me." Kyle ran back inside and stuffed the half-empty water bottle into the backpack.

"Never mind the water. We need to move fast, and want to carry as little as possible," Gareth said and pulled the blanket off the cot. He cut a hole in the center with the knife, fashioning it into a poncho. "Now, put on my jacket," he urged. He helped Kyle pull up the zipper and draw the hood over his head.

Kyle mused. *He must have children. Dad used to zip up my zipper and tighten my hood when I was little.* Kyle met Gareth's eyes.

"What is it? Are you worried?"

"You remind me of my dad."

"I bet he doesn't look like me."

"No," he shook his head. "Not on the outside. I still miss him."

"What happened to him?" Gareth pulled the poncho over his head.

"He died. A heart attack."

"I'm sorry." Gareth grabbed the backpack. "Ready?"

They left the shed and headed back down the way Gareth had come. Snow fell steadily now. Quietness surrounded them, except for the crunching of their footsteps on the frozen earth and occasional clumps of snow thumping to the ground as the wind flogged the tree branches.

"I can't hear the helicopter," Kyle said. His breathing had grown heavy, louder. In spite of the freezing temperatures, beads of perspiration appeared on his face. Gareth stood next to him, snow clinging to his eyebrows. He stared at the sky.

"They've given up, I'm sure. The visibility is poor." He looked at Kyle. "You okay?"

"Yes, I'm fine. Let's go." Kyle trudged forward. Gareth followed. The weakened state of the boy worried him, but the farther away from the shed they got, the better their chances of escaping other wolves and being rescued. *As soon as the sky provides an opening, I could shoot off another flare. Trouble is, only two flares left, and I'd better use them wisely.*

———

"Let's try one more time," the pilot said. He widened the circles while his partner focused the binoculars on the slopes below. The snow still fell heavily. A sudden unexpected opening in the cloud cover revealed snow-covered trees and low growing brush, but no sign of life.

"I'm running low on fuel. Let's give it one more whirl, and then we've gotta head back."

Below, Gareth again heard the whooping of the helicopter's blades.

"It's the chopper," Kyle said. He leaned against a tree and slowly slid down to the ground. *I'm dead tired. I need some sleep.* His head fell forward.

"Kyle, look!" Gareth fumbled with the backpack. He fired the flare just as the opening in the cloud cover began to close. Kyle did not respond. Gareth rushed toward him.

"They have to see this one."

Kyler blinked and nodded and closed his eyes again.

Gareth shook him gently. "Kyle, wake up. We've got to get moving." He grabbed Kyle's shoulders and pulled him up. "I'm sure they spotted the flare. They'll send help. I know it. Come on; put your arm around my neck." He grabbed Kyle's waist with his right hand and dragged him along. Kyle's feet refused to obey. Partially numb, they felt like jelly.

"A flare, to your left."

"I see it," the pilot said. "Radio for help. Looks like he's on his way down the mountain." He circled a few more times, but a grey swirling mass of blowing snow blocked any view. "Let's return to base."

———◆———

CHAPTER 32

"SARGE," THE DESK CLERK APPROACHED Bilko's office. He waved him inside. "Sarge," the man said, "we just got a radio message. The chopper has spotted a flare halfway down the mountain.

"That's him." Bilko pushed his chair back. "That's the detective. He told me he bought flares. Let's get the rescue team together. We've got to go up there. Now."

"The chopper is coming back. Fuel's running out."

"That's fine. They wouldn't be able to land up there in this stuff even if there was a level opening." Bilko slipped into his coat, snatched his hat and brushed by the clerk.

"Can we stop for a minute?" Kyle disengaged Gareth's arms and sank to the ground. "I need to rest." He swept his hand through the snow, gathered a fistful, and shoved it into his mouth.

Gareth glanced at the exhausted boy and nodded. He could do with a break as well. He flexed his arms and took a deep breath as he watched Kyle suck on the snow. *Be strong, Kyle. You've been through hell, but we're almost home.*

"Do you think they saw the flare?" Kyle said between swallows.

"I can't be sure. There's a strong possibility; nevertheless, assuming they didn't see it, we have to keep going and get out of here. If there are more wolves, they'll have no problem tracking us. We won't stand a chance against a pack of wolves."

Kyle didn't answer. If only he weren't so tired. All he cared about at this point was getting some sleep. His lids hung heavily across his eyes. He didn't have the energy to raise them. His dad's face floated in front of his closed eyes. *Dad, are you with God? Are you coming to meet me?* He raised a weak arm to touch his father's cheek.

"Kyle, wake up. Let's go."

"I can't, I'm just going to stay here."

"Like hell you are." Gareth pulled him up.

Kyle turned his head. "Leave me here. I can't go on."

"Yes, you can. Come on, put your arm around me and let's go." He kept talking while dragging Kyle along. "I *know* they saw the flare. They'll send help. I'm sure of it. We've got to keep moving."

Move, like putting one foot in front of the other. I can do it. I want to live. I want to take many more photos. Dad, I want you to be proud of me. God, please help me. Kyle planted his feed firmly on the ground and dragged one in front of the other.

Gareth smiled at him, "That's it. You're doing great, Kyle."

They passed a large pine tree. The wolf jumped out from beneath the brush surrounding it, sunk his teeth into Kyle's left leg, and tried to drag him into the bushes. Kyle opened his mouth, but the scream stuck in his throat. He fell forward and clawed frantically at the ground, at the same time, Gareth raised his revolver and shot the wolf in what he hoped was the lungs or the heart. The beast gave a whimper and then lay still.

The ambulance came to a halt, along with the police emergency vehicle. Bilko and the men got out. Snow fell steadily from the sky, obstructing visibility and making the uphill climb more hazardous. One of the officers had a stretcher strapped to his back. All of them carried rifles.

"Go, go, go." Bilko said, and the three took off while Bilko and the driver of the ambulance stayed behind. In less than an hour the men reached the accident scene, now completely covered with snow. They traversed in silence at a steady pace across rock slabs covered with thin ice. The trail then curved to the left, dropped briefly, and then rose.

They heard the wolves' high pitched calls. As one, they took the rifles from their shoulders, keeping the steady pace. They were rangers who knew the terrain and were trained to deal with the hazards—whether beast or weather—of a mountain rescue.

The shot rang through the forest. "Sounds like a sidearm," one of the men said.

"Straight ahead," another replied, pointing his head upward. Their breaths filled the air with opaque vapors.

Gareth kneeled next to Kyle. "Let me take a look." He examined the leg. The bite-marks located on the side of Kyle's calf had penetrated his jeans, and blood trickled through the torn opening. Kyle moaned as Gareth moved the pants leg up. Two puncture wounds oozed a steady stream of blood. He searched the backpack. He never left the house without adding a small first aid kit to his gear, and he thanked God that he did so this time as well. He located it and bandaged the wound expertly. He looked up and saw the wolves. Three adult animals stood across the clearing snarling and baring their teeth.

"Gareth, look!"

"Hush. Don't look into their eyes and don't move."

Gareth checked out the tree. One of them could make it up there. "Kyle, can you climb that tree?" The words left his mouth through gritted teeth.

"I think so."

"Go!" Gareth said just as the wolves charged them. Gareth gave Kyle a push, and he quickly moved up to a higher level. Gareth fired and missed. The wolves continued to run toward him, and he fired again. One of them yelped, and all three retreated. Gareth holstered his gun, reached for the branch, and swung his legs up. Breathing heavily, he climbed up. His arms wrapped around the tree trunk, he dropped his forehead against the tree. His heart beat like a drum, and he couldn't remember a time when he had been more scared.

The wolves below recovered and attacked the tree, jumping high and growling at Gareth's heels.

"Shoot them," Kyle yelled from above him. "Why don't you shoot them?"

"I only have two bullets left," Gareth said. "We're safe for now."

The noise subsided, and Gareth moved one of the branches to the side and glanced below. The wolves had disappeared; picked up the scent of an elk or red deer Gareth guessed. "How is the leg?" he asked.

"All right. Hurts like hell." Kyle paused for a moment and then added under his breath, "I wish I had my camera."

"This is a fine time to think about taking pictures." Gareth raised his head and listened as the wind whistled around his ears. "Kyle, the wolves are gone," he said.

Kyle tightened his grip. His leg throbbed. "Is it safe to leave?"

"I'm not sure."

They heard the voices at the same time.

"Help!" they both cried.

Kyle, having the better vantage point, was the first to see the men come around the bend. "Here!! We're over here!" He waved, and the tree began to shake dropping bunches of snow.

Gareth had already lowered himself to the ground. He looked up at Kyle and asked, "Can you make it?"

"Sure thing." Kyle proceeded to climb down.

One of the men checked him out, while the other joined Gareth staring at the dead wolf.

"Looks like we got here in time," the man said.

"I must admit, there have been some tense moments. God, I'm glad to see you." Gareth reached out his hand. "Gareth Morton, and this is Kyle Weldon." They walked over to the tree.

"Ranger Ed Brown, and these are my partners, rangers Sam Lackland and Mark Duncan. Sam's a medic," he pointed to the man kneeling next to Kyle. Sam nodded and rose.

"Kyle is okay. The wounds are not serious, but he may need rabies vaccination." Kyle rolled his eyes and remained silent. He wasn't looking forward to the painful injections.

Sam turned the wolf over.

"You're going to cut off his head?" Kyle said.

"Yes, the lab needs to check the brain to see if the animal has been infected with rabies."

Ed brought up the stretcher. "Here, let's get you comfortable so we can get going. We have an ambulance waiting at the bottom of the mountain."

"I'm okay," Kyle protested.

"Sorry, procedure. We've got to take you to the hospital. Once the laboratory results are available, the doctor will decide if you need the rabies vaccination."

"How long will that take?"

"A few days." Ed tucked the blanket around Kyle and motioned to Mark to get ready to pick up one end of the stretcher. "Are you about done, Sam?"

"Yes." Sam tied the plastic bag holding the remains of the wolf's head. "Ready," he said. Ed and Mark picked up the stretcher, and Gareth followed. The snowfall began to pick up and lightly dusted Kyle. The sky had slipped beneath a blanket of dreary grey that hung ominously above the small group laboring their way down the mountain.

CHAPTER 33

———————◆———————

"MRS. WELDON? RICHARD SLOAN."

Joan's grip tensed on the receiver.

"I've got good news. I just heard from Gareth; they've found Kyle. He's alive and well."

"Thank God," she pressed her fist against her mouth as she dropped onto the kitchen chair. Tears streamed down her face; she couldn't stop sobbing.

Richard Sloan wiped away a tear or two of his own. He could only imagine what this poor woman had suffered. He felt her pain and gave her time to release. The joy would come soon enough.

Joan wept in silence. She dropped the receiver and rose to get the tissue box from the counter.

Richard heard the commotion and waited patiently. When she came back on the line she said, "I'm sorry, Mr. Sloan. I'm just overwhelmed."

"I know. So am I. I'm driving up to Sheffield to see Kyle. He's in the local hospital for observation. I want to swing by and pick you up. I'll fill you in on all the details on the way."

When she didn't answer, he urged, "I want to take you to see Kyle. I'm here, at the *Graceville Register.* I can be at your house in a few minutes."

"I heard you. I'll be ready."

He smiled. She had rallied. What a brave woman.

"I can't wait to hear all about what happened to Kyle. I want to know every detail. Hurry." She hung up. She scribbled a brief note for Luke, who was still at school, and taped it to the refrigerator. She knew he would be upset at not being able to go, but she couldn't worry about his feelings now. She had to see Kyle, make sure he's all right. *Oh God, thank you for keeping him safe.* She slipped into her coat, grabbed her purse, and left the house. She skipped down the steps and ran toward the front of the driveway, where she paced impatiently until Richard's car pulled beside her.

"Nurse," he called impatiently. "Nurse, please, can I get dressed now?" Kyle sat on the edge of the bed, his left leg sporting a bandage. The pain was minimal. He wanted to leave, go outside, smell fresh air, and revel in the fact he was alive. How good it was to be free and warm, and to have a full stomach. His fingers were itching to write his story. Although he didn't have any photos, he could always return to Marshall Point Lighthouse and take more photos. As a matter of fact, he would enjoy visiting the area again, even if it has to be at his own expense. His thoughts ran through a gamut of ideas. He had so much to tell. Now, that he was safe, he could talk about his experience with sincerity. The emotions could not be more real.

"Kyle!"

Joan dashed through the door. She wrapped her arms around him so tightly he protested. "Mom, I can't breathe."

She released her grip but didn't let go. "I've been so worried."

His mouth next to her ear, he whispered, "Mom, I'm all right. Really."

She dropped her arms and stepped back. Her eyes fell on the bandage, and then met his. "The wolf?" she asked, and he nodded.

Richard Sloan stepped up and gave Kyle a bear hug. "It's good to see you. How are you feeling?"

Kyle leaned back. Seeing Richard Sloan surprised him. "I'm fine. I want to get out of here. Look," he jumped off the bed and limped around the room. "See I can walk. I'm bored stiff in here. I need to get back to work." He brought his hand up to his forehead and shook his head. "I forgot my camera equipment is gone." He turned to Joan, "Mom, what am I going to do?"

"Leave it up to me," Richard said. "You concentrate on getting well so you can soon return to Portland to resume your job."

"Portland?" Joan interjected. "He needs to rest. I want him to come home to Graceville." She saw Kyle's grimace and quickly added, "At least, for a little while."

"I think we can arrange it." Richard said. "Kyle, why don't you take a few days off before you return to Portland?"

Kyle nodded. He had no intentions of resting. He intended get started on his story right away. At one point, he planned to visit Mt. Blue and take some photos there.

Joan suppressed a smile. He really was okay. A little pale and a little thinner, but they had much to be thankful for. During the drive from Graceville to Sheffield, Richard Sloan filled her in on the details of Kyle's ordeal, and she was horrified. She asked a lot of questions. Thanks to Gareth's detailed report, Richard was able to answer most of them. He also assured her Kyle's name would be cleared, which was the reason he had seen the owner of the *Graceville Register,* a friend of his. Before he left, he had instructed his editors at the *Portland Journal* to do the same.

A young girl came into the room carrying a tray. "Dinner," she said. Kyle lifted the lids: Chicken stew, fruit salad and wheat toast.

He frowned and Joan said, "Is he allowed to have outside food?"

The girl grinned. "He can have anything he wants," she said, "except alcohol." She placed the tray in front of Kyle and left the room.

"I believe I saw a MacDonald's across the street," Richard said, and Kyle's eyes lit up. Both Joan and Kyle gave Richard their orders. "Be right back," he announced over his shoulder and left the room. He nearly collided with Sergeant Bilko.

"I beg your pardon." Bilko stepped aside. Richard nodded and hurried down the hallway.

"How's the patient doing?" Bilko walked up to the bed and placed a canvas bag on it. "Sergeant Bilko, Sheffield Police Department." He extended his hand to Kyle and then to Joan.

"Glad to meet you, Ma'am."

"Likewise," Joan said as she studied the burly man. *He doesn't look like Sergeant Bilko.* She suppressed a smile.

"What's in the bag?" Kyle asked.

"Take a look," Bilko said.

Kyle dragged it next to him and reached inside. His eyes lit up. He took a quick, sharp breath and pulled out his camera. "Wow," he said and his eyes got misty. "My dad bought me this camera. I thought I'd never see it again." He examined it closely. "It looks okay."

"A pawnshop owner in Farmington brought it to the station once the story got out you were missing. He read about the case and he realized this could be your camera. He didn't want to be accused of receiving stolen goods. After I printed the photos on the memory card, I was certain it was yours."

Kyle, speechless, just nodded.

"Then all you need to do is sign here."

Kyle signed the paper and looked up at Bilko. "Thank you so much. You don't know what this means to me." His jaw set, he added, "Now all I need is permission to leave this place."

"I can do that for you." The doctor appeared from behind Bilko.

"I'll be going," Bilko said and again shook Kyle's hand. "Lots of luck to you." He turned to Joan. *What an attractive woman.* Visions of Emily, his wife, shot through his head, and he flinched. *What am I thinking?* He bowed to Joan, and with a twinkle in his eye he said, "Take care of that boy."

Joan nodded and watched him leave.

"Mrs. Weldon," the doctor said.

She didn't answer.

"Mrs. Weldon?"

"Oh, I'm sorry. Daydreaming, I guess."

"That's quite all right. We're releasing Kyle. We'll contact him once we have the lab report, and if the animal was infected, he will need to see a local doctor to obtain rabies vaccine."

Her eyes widened.

"He may not need it," he assured her, "but we must be certain."

Richard arrived with the food, and Kyle ate with gusto. During the drive home to Graceville, he spent the entire time sleeping in the back seat of Richard's car, clutching the canvas bag holding his camera.

CHAPTER 34

———◆———

DRESSED IN A WARM FLEECE hoodie, Kyle walked the beach. The surf ploughed the sand with foaming crests that coiled back like dappled serpents. The sun fought to peek through the clouds and erratic shafts of bright light stabbed at Kyle. He raised his camera and captured two gulls in flight fighting over a catch.

"Kyle."

He turned and saw Joan standing on the deck waving frantically. "Kyle!"

He hurried up to the house and saw the worried look on her face. "What is it?"

He stood next to her catching his breath.

"A physician from Sheffield General Hospital called. The test results were positive. You must see our doctor right away to begin the rabies vaccinations."

"Great. From what I hear, they're no fun."

"I know." She tugged on his arm. "You have no choice. I've already phoned Dr. McNamara. He'll see you tomorrow morning at nine o'clock."

They stepped into the kitchen. Luke was eating breakfast and reading the paper. He raised the front page and stuck it into Kyle's face. "Here, big brother, they cleared your name."

"Cleared my name?"

"Why, yes…"

Joan silenced Luke with a stern look and reached for the paper. "For a little while, but only a little while, you were the murder suspect in the death of the woman at the gift shop at Marshall Point," she said.

"Me, a killer?" Kyle dropped onto the chair. "But it was the creep who kidnapped me. He was the murderer, and he would have killed me too if..." *Everyone who knows me is aware that I couldn't kill anyone. I gave my statement to the police when they came to the hospital in Sheffield.* He reached for the paper and began to read the headline, "Local Man cleared of Murder Charges."

Luke slapped his back, "You're famous, brother."

Kyle didn't reply but kept reading. Based on an interview the journalist had with Gareth, the article covered everything from the moment he discovered the killer in the gift shop to his experiences on the mountain.

Joan sat down next to Kyle. "Your name is cleared now. They know you didn't do it. Are you all right, Kyle?" Joan's voice trembled. "I know you went through a terrible ordeal. I thank God every night he gave you back to us alive. I've been so worried, so worried..." she broke down

"Mom, it's okay." He squeezed her hand. "I'm fine, really. No need to worry."

She raised her eyes to his, straightened her shoulders, and said. "I know. I'd like to meet Gareth and thank him in person for what he did for you."

Kyle answered with a shrug. His phone rang and he answered.

"Kyle. It's Lisa."

"Hello."

"Kyle, it's so good to hear your voice. I've... everyone has been so worried about you. Thank God you're safe." She rambled on, and he interrupted her.

"I'm glad you called. You've been on my mind a lot." He looked at Joan and Luke before stepping out on the deck.

"I've had lots of time to think, Lisa."

"Have you? About us?" When he didn't answer she added, "Can I come to see you?"

"I'm driving up to Marshall Point in a little while to pick up my belongings."

"Oh," she said.

"Do you want to come along?"

"Yes, yes. Can I bring Andy?"

"Of course. Can you be ready in an hour?"

"We'll be ready."

He returned to the kitchen. "I'm driving to Marshall Point. Lisa is coming with me," he said. He strolled out of the kitchen and up the stairs whistling.

"Listen," Luke said

"Yes, I know. He always whistles when he's happy." Joan poured another cup of coffee and began reading the newspaper article for the third time, looking proudly at the photo of her handsome son.

Kyle parked the rental car and looked up at the gift shop. A large red and white sign announced the gift shop was temporarily closed. He wiped his eyes as if to erase the images of Melanie's body.

"Mom, can I go up to the lighthouse?" Andy pulled on the restraining belt of his car seat.

"Why don't you take him up to the platform, and I'll join you shortly?" Kyle said.

"Sure thing. Come, Andy." Lisa had already exited the car and lifted Andy from the back seat. He immediately grabbed her hand and pulled her across the wooden bridge, as Kyle watched. *He calls her Mom.* He had to get used to the idea that she would be Andy's mother soon. His feelings for her had changed, and she occupied his mind a great deal. He knew she was in love with him, but how did he feel about her? He had discovered that spending time with her had become very important to him. During the drive to Marshall Point, he had repeatedly reached for her hand. It felt comfortable in his. He headed for the stairs leading to the apartment.

"Mom, look at the big birds," Andy cried.

"They're sea gulls, sweetheart." She had an iron grip on his hand, eliminating any attempts he made to disengage.

"Mr. Kyle!" he craned his neck and waved. Wind gusts battered his little body. He loved it.

Kyle stopped at the landing. "Don't get blown away."

"I won't. Mom's keeping me safe."

Kyles smiled and stepped into the apartment. A quick glance told him nothing had changed. The dirty coffee cup still sat on the kitchen table, and pieces of clothing littered the floor. He quickly picked them up and stuffed everything inside the duffel bag he'd brought with him. He cleaned up the kitchen and emptied the refrigerator. He located a bag of dried bread and took it with him as he left the apartment. Before shutting the door, he took a last look around. *I'm not the same person who stayed here before. Maybe that's a good thing.* His eyes wandered to the lighthouse. The sun had slipped through the clouds. His heart skipped a beat as he watched the woman and the boy, and he knew they were his future. He ran down the stairs, deposited the duffel bag into the trunk of the car, and walked confidently across the bridge, waving the bag containing the bread.

Taking two steps at a time, he climbed to the top. Andy and Lisa waited at the platform. He picked up Andy, pulled Lisa into his arms and kissed her. Her lips felt soft and inviting. He didn't want to release them, but Andy pushed against him. Kyle whispered into her ear, "We'll have to take this up later." He put Andy down, and together they began feeding the sea gulls that dove into the sea with uncanny precision and rose with their prize only to be chased by their comrades.

Andy yelled and jumped as he fed the birds. His little cheeks were red and his hair windblown. Then the bread was gone. They lingered for a few moments longer until Kyle said, "We'd better leave." He picked up Andy and carried him down the steps. Lisa followed. As soon as they reached the bridge he deposited Andy on his feet, and the little boy took off. His little legs flew across the decking, and he threw his arms up into the air, stretching them wide, "Look Mom, I'm an airplane!"

"I see. Don't fly too fast," Lisa warned.

Kyle pulled her close and kissed her on the cheek. She leaned against him. Joy lit up her eyes. *He loves me. He's loved me all along; he just didn't know it. If only he could say the words.* She looked up at his handsome face. A feeling of weightlessness overcame her, and she felt light as a feather.

They arrived at the car. Lisa called Andy, and Kyle deposited him securely into the car seat and then turned to Lisa, "Buckle your seatbelt," he said.

"Yes, sir."

Kyle closed the passenger door and straightened up. Marshall Point Light stood proud against the setting sun. The seagulls screeched as they sailed low above the water, and the thundering tide beat against the shore. The same pattern over and over again, an eon of unrelenting assault.

CHAPTER 35

———◆———

KYLE STOPPED THE CAR IN front of Lisa's parents' house on Acadia Avenue. Andy had been asleep for the last hour. His head rested to one side, his mouth open. Kyle reached for Lisa's hand, turned it over, and kissed her palm. She brought the other hand up to his face and drew him near. The kiss, long and deep, left no doubt about their shared feelings. When Kyle finally released her mouth he cupped her face and whispered, "I'm in love with you, Lisa."

She looked deeply into his eyes and replied, "You already know how I feel about you. My feelings have never changed, Kyle."

He nodded and said, "I don't deserve you." He looked down. "I've been looking at life through a tainted lens when I thought I loved Amy." He pressed his cheek against hers. "I see things clearly now. I'm a lucky guy."

"We're both lucky." Her smile broadened into laughter, and he joined her. Andy opened his eyes. He looked at the two silly adults for a moment and then demanded to have his seatbelt undone. He was ready to see Granny and tell her about his adventures.

"Mom, open the door," he urged. Lisa reluctantly disengaged her hand from Kyle's and exited the car. The front door opened, and Lisa's mom stepped out of the house. Andy bolted up the steps, right into her arms and she swung him around.

"Granny, I saw a lighthouse today, and millions and a thousand sea gulls. And I fed them too!"

"Did you now?" Granny said. "Looks like you had a busy day." She waved to Kyle who stood next to Lisa, and took Andy inside. At this moment, Andy came back out, hurrying down the steps with his arms wide open. "Thank you, Mr. Kyle."

Kyle picked him up and gave him a hug. "You're very welcome. I'll see you soon, Andy."

"Yes, sir." Andy scrambled up the steps and ran into the house,

"I like that kid," Kyle said.

"Do you? You know the adoption will be final in a few weeks."

"I'm happy for you, Lisa. It's a wonderful thing you're doing."

She chewed on her lower lip as he watched. She opened her mouth to speak, but he said, "Will you allow me to be around to help you raise him?"

Her eyes searched his face, while her heart beat rose.

He nodded encouragingly and she said, "You mean, be his daddy?"

"Yes, that's exactly what I mean." He held her close. He lifted up her chin and saw the tears. "No more tears, Lisa," he said. "I love you with all my heart and I want to spend the rest of my life with you and Andy."

She closed her eyes and placed her arms around him. "Just hold me close, Kyle, real close."

Kyle left the doctor's office. He had already endured his first dose of rabies anti-toxin. Now, he had his second one today. Two more to go. His leg almost healed, he planned to go back to work the day after tomorrow. He had put additional finishing touches on the Marshall Point assignment and mailed it to Conley Brown, the editor of the *Portland Journal.* He saw Lisa almost every night. He had made up his mind, but had not asked her to marry him yet. He wanted to become more established in his field. He needed a steady income before he could take on a wife and son.

"Hello."

"Kyle, how are you?" Richard Sloan's voice echoed through the phone.

"Terrific. My leg is fully healed."

"Are you ready for a new assignment?"

A soft gasp escaped his lips. "Ready? Yes!"

"I wanted to make sure you're fully recovered before I send you out into the world."

Kyle's ears perked up. "I'm listening."

"How good is your German?"

"My German?" Kyle was confused. "I've had four years of it, so I'm pretty fluent, I guess."

"Good. You're going to Helgoland."

"Helgoland?"

"Yes. German is the official language spoken there. Do you know where it is?"

Kyle's eyes sparkled, and he spoke rapidly. "It's a small archipelago in the North Sea."

Richard chuckled. Only Conley, the editor at the paper, knew the details about this island. Few of his crew knew exactly where it was located, and Conley immediately began educating them.

"Then you know about it. It has a fascinating history. I want you to delve into it in your article. The strategic importance during several wars dates back to the 19th century. Take lots of pictures."

"Yes, Sir. When do I leave?"

"Next week, providing you've got a passport."

"I do. My whole family got passports when Dad took us to Canada the year I graduated from high school-right before he died." Kyle bounced lightly in place. *Next week. Might as well be next year. How do I get through this week?*

"Good."

"I think I'm going to head straight for the library." He checked his watch. He had enough time.

"Good. Learn as much as you can about the island. Nikki will book your flight. Stop by the paper and pick up your assignment details and a credit card for your expenses. If there is anything else you need, let me know."

"Okay. Bye, Mr. Sloan, and thanks so much." Kyle disconnected, reached for his coat and hurried out the door almost colliding with Joan. He swung her around and lifted her into the air while she let out a short laugh.

"Hey, what's gotten into you?" She stared at him with open mouth.

"Mom, I'm the happiest man alive. I'm going to Helgoland." He put her down, pecked her cheek, and dashed out the door.

"Wait a minute. Where are you going...?" The words lingered in the air as she watched him climb into the car and head down the driveway. "And where in the world is Helgoland?" She added.

———————

"Check please," Kyle said to the waiter. The music through the intercom was playing "Only You," a popular song from the fifties. He reached across the table and took Lisa's hand. "Happy?"

"Yes." She looked around. "This is a lovely place, quiet and elegant."

He nodded. Because he was leaving the country shortly, he had arranged a weekend trip to New York City. As excited as he was about the assignment, the thought of leaving Lisa was tough. They saw each other every day, and he had fallen deeply in love with her. On those rare occasions, when he thought about Amy these days, he compared her to Lisa and realized what a fool he'd been. Lisa was lovely and honest and faithful. She told him they were soul mates, and he was beginning to understand what she meant. They hadn't made love yet because he wanted it to be a very special moment.

"Ready?"

"Yes," she said and rose.

Holding hands, they left the restaurant. The doorman called a taxi which took them to the Belvedere Hotel on 48th Street. He had taken her to Broadway to see *Les Miserables* earlier that day. They sat close together, and he noticed her tears as the sad story unfolded. The bittersweet music even stirred his emotions.

They got off the elevator, and he fumbled for the key. When he dropped it, she quickly picked it up, opened the door, and walked inside. He stood still until she reached out her hand and pulled him into the luxurious room. She dropped her purse onto the night table and took off her jacket. He stood and watched her, and she came toward him. He took her into his arms and crushed her to him. His kiss was slow, thoughtful. His tongue traced the soft fullness of her lips.

"Oh Kyle," she moaned and dropped her head back. His mouth traveled down her neck and to the cleavage of her dress. As he roused her passion, his own grew stronger. His hand moved to her back and pulled down the zipper. She wiggled, and the dress fell to the floor. His hand outlined the circle of her breast. The gentle caress sent currents of desire through her. Holding him close, she inched her way to the bed and sat down. He took her hands and kissed both palms, then stepped aside, and got naked. When he turned, she had slipped between the sheets, her clothes scattered on the floor. He slid in next to her, and his lips sought hers. She drank in the sweetness of his kiss.

"Lisa," he said, his mouth close to her face. "I love you. I want to be with you always. Let's get married as soon as I return from Helgoland. Let's not wait."

"Yes, yes…" Tears welled in her eyes. *This was not a moment for tears.* "Make love to me, Kyle," she whispered, and pulled him close.

CHAPTER 36

———◆———

THE CHIME ANNOUNCED THE PILOT turned on the fasten seatbelt sign. Kyle opened his eyes and looked out the window. Soon he would land in Cuxhaven from there he planned to take the catamaran for the 70 km ride across the North Sea to the red isle of Helgoland.

The vessel sped across the water as the island came into view. Kyle pulled up his collar and inhaled deeply. The air smelled of sea and salt. He heard the wind sing a sweet song as the surf pounded the shore. In the distance, Lange Anna, the landmark of Helgoland rose. A strange red rock giant on the Northern tip of the island, it bordered the Lummenfelsen, the world's smallest nature preserve. He raised his camera and clicked. Spray dotted the lens. He wiped it dry and returned the camera to its case.

After disembarking the catamaran, Kyle reveled in the mild temperatures. Snow was on the ground when he left Maine and the temperatures seemed frozen in the teens. He'd read about Helgoland's mild temperatures, incongruous but furnished graciously by the surrounding Gulf Stream, which provided bright but not too hot summer seasons and ensured the exotic plants covering the island did not get frost bitten—even in mid-winter.

Kyle picked up his luggage and headed for the Unterland where his hotel was located. Along the way, he stopped many times, taking photos of the Binnenhafen (the harbor), the many shops housed in clapboard row-houses painted bright blue, orange, red and yellow, and quaint local pubs offering outdoor seating. *What an amazing place. I've never seen anything like it. I can't wait to explore the island.*

He reached Hotel Fallersleben. The friendly receptionist spoke English. The official language was German, but the natives used mostly Halunder, the island language. His room offered a fantastic view of the sea. He dropped onto the comfortable bed and stretched. He realized he hadn't slept in over 24 hours, but there was so much to do. He turned to his side and closed his eyes.

He woke to a dark room and a growling stomach. He washed up and headed downstairs for the dining room.

The car flew across the icy road and slowed dramatically, its rear wheels spinning as it approached the salt truck. A curse escaped Luke's lips as he checked the speedometer-40 miles an hour. *Why does he drive so slowly? There's hardly any ice on the road. Well, no sweat, I'll be turning off this highway soon.* He approached the fork and turned left, entering the road leading to his house, without using his signal, giving the unsuspecting driver of the truck the finger. He chuckled. *Mom would have a fit if she saw me.* He pulled into the driveway.

Dressed in boots and anorak, her hood tightly pulled over her head, Joan wielded the broom clearing the snow off her car. Luke came to a stop beside her, just as another car pulled into the driveway.

"Why, it's Vince," Joan said.

"I tried to call you. No one answered," Vince said and slammed the car door. He turned to Luke and said in a low tone, "You're in a bit of a hurry this morning. You can get killed driving that way." He gave him a stern look and turned to Joan.

"I've been out here for the last hour. I'm having a hard time clearing the ice off the windshield." She put down the scraper and smiled at him. "Did you come to get me?"

"Yes, since you insisted on coming in, I thought I'd better give you a ride." He winked at her, and she gave him a bear hug. He glanced above her head at Luke who watched with interest. "I told you the books can wait," Vince added.

"I go crazy being in the house. There's only so much housework to be done. I'm looking forward to a day at your office." She handed Luke the scraper and the broom and grabbed her purse sitting on the passenger seat. "Let's go." She waved to Luke and said jokingly, "Don't wait up for me."

Vince opened the car door for her and she slipped inside. "See you, Luke." He tipped his cap and got into the car. He started the engine then turned to Joan and grabbed her hand and kissed it. "Don't you think it's time to tell the boys we're planning to get married?"

"I guess I'm just worried how they'll take it."

"Do you think they don't like me?"

"No, it's not that. They've known you forever. Let's wait until Kyle gets back from Helgoland. We'll make the announcement then."

"Whatever you say, my love." He leaned over and kissed her. Joan buckled her seatbelt as they pulled into the road.

"I've got some great news. Richard Sloan called me. He's been approached by someone from *National Geographic Magazine*. They want to use Kyle's photos for an article on the homeless in America. Isn't it exciting?" Joan said.

"That's fantastic! What an opportunity! Wow, to be featured in this great magazine. This will give him worldwide exposure. What did Kyle say?"

"I haven't told him yet. I thought I wait until he gets home next week." She paused and turned to Vince. "We'll have two surprises for Kyle." She smiled and leaned her head against his shoulder.

Kyle packed his suitcase. He seemed to be running out of room. He had bought souvenirs for everyone. T-shirts and mugs featuring the tri-color Helgoland flag with three horizontal bars, from top to bottom: green, red and white, for Joan, Luke, and Lisa, and a wooden replica of a German battleship dating from 1918 for Andy. He pulled the zipper and checked his watch. He had three more hours to go before he boarded the plane, a last minute decision, for the trip included an aerial tour of the two islands and the pilot promised there would be many opportunities to take photos from the air.

He had bumped into Helmut Kullmann, the pilot, two days ago when he was shopping in the Oberland. Kyle asked him for directions to the Seeblick Restaurant where he planned to have lunch; the receptionist at the hotel had recommended it. She spoke in German and since his was a bit rusty he didn't follow her completely. He thanked her profusely and left, trusting his instincts to find the place.

"Ah, you're an American. Come, I'll show you. It's not far," Helmut had said. To Kyle's surprise, Helmut spoke perfect English. What a relief.

"I spent a year in your country," Helmut said. "South Carolina. I have a cousin there. I enjoyed myself, but the summers were hot as hell. How do you people stand it?"

Kyle looked at Helmut's shock of blond hair; his eyes matched the crystal clear blue sky above. He was at least six feet tall.

"I'm from Maine," Kyle said. "Our summers are much more tolerable and our winters are long."

"You should move to Helgoland. The climate here is perfect."

"I've noticed," Kyle said and laughed. "The island is beautiful. I haven't been to the Duene, the smaller island, yet."

"You have to see it." Pointing at the camera around Kyle's neck, Helmut said, "You must capture it on film. Are you a professional photographer?"

"I'm a photojournalist. I'm here on assignment. What do you do here?" Kyle asked.

"I'm a pilot. I have a small plane available for charter flights around the islands as well as roundtrips to the mainland."

Kyle's ears perked up "I'm leaving in two days. Would you be available to take me on a sightseeing tour and then continue to the mainland?"

Helmut pulled out a small date book and leafed through it. He looked up. "Yes, I can do it on Friday. Where are you staying?"

"Hotel Fallersleben."

"Ah," Helmut nodded and sighed. "August Heinrich Hoffmann von Fallersleben is my favorite poet." He paused.

Kyle pulled out his notebook. "Go on," he said. "What's his connection with Helgoland?"

"In 1841 von Fallersleben visited Helgoland, a British possession at the time. On the boat trip to the island, the ship's band played the Marsellaise to honor the French passengers, followed by God Save the King to honor their British guests. Von Fallersleben was a German patriot and resented his country being snubbed. As soon as he landed on the island, he began writing *"Das Lied der Deutschen,"* (A German Song), based on a musical composition by Joseph Haydn. The date was August 26, 1841. How could he ever imagine his work would become the National Anthem of Germany?"

Kyle put down his notebook. "Amazing." They had arrived at the Seeblick. "Look," Kyle said, "why don't you have lunch with me? Do you have the time?"

Helmut checked his watch. "Of course, I'd like that."

They found a table and sat down. After they placed their orders, Helmut said, "Helgoland has an interesting history. It is known to have been inhabited since prehistoric times. In 697, Radbod, the last Frisian king, retreated to the island after being defeated by the Franks. By 1231, the island was listed as the property of the Danish king Valdemar II."

Their drinks arrived, mugs filled with the full-bodied German beer Kyle had learned to appreciate since he arrived. They toasted and Helmut continued. "During the next four centuries ownership of the islands switched several times between Denmark and the Duchy of Schleswig until it remained Danish in 1807.

"Through the Napoleonic Wars, Helgoland became a center of smuggling and espionage against Napoleon and eventually capitulated to the British. In 1814, Denmark formally ceded Helgoland to the United Kingdom." Helmut paused and raised his eyebrows. "Are you tired of hearing me talk yet?"

Kyle shook his head emphatically. "Not at all. Please go on. This is fascinating. I hope you don't mind if I quote you in my article."

"Go right ahead. History is my hobby, and Helgoland's history is colorful indeed."

"When did the Germans take over the islands?"

"Britain gave up the islands to Germany in 1890. The newly unified country was concerned about a foreign power controlling a strategic point that could command the western entrance to the militarily-important Kiel Canal in Germany.

"Soon after, Helgoland developed into a seaside spa attracting much of the Hanoverian upper-class. Artists and writers visited, especially from Germany and even Austria.

"Under the German empire, the islands became a major naval base. During the First World War, the civilian population was evacuated to the mainland." Helmut took the last bite of his sandwich and added, "It may be of interest to the Americans to learn that Helgoland played an important part during World War I and II."

Kyle nodded while he completed his notes. He looked up. "I plan to get married soon," he said.

"Congratulations!" Helmut grinned widely.

"This would be the ideal place to spend a honeymoon." Kyle looked around. "Yes, I think Lisa would love it."

"Be sure to look me up when you come." Helmut pushed back his chair and rose. "You may want to stop at one of the local book stores. Helgoland's history during World War II is fascinating. After the evacuation, the islands remained uninhabited from 1945 to 1952. On March 1, 1952 the former residents were allowed to return to their homes. The first of March is an official holiday on the islands." He zipped up his jacket and said, "Well, I've got to run."

"Thanks for the history lesson," Kyle said and stood up. They shook hands.

"Don't mention it. See you on Friday. Meet me at the Duene Island airport at 8:00 A.M. You take the ferry from here. Do you know where to catch it?"

"I'll find it. See you then."

Helmut nodded, smiled, and left.

CHAPTER 37

—◆—

"LUKE, WHAT ARE YOU DOING here?"

Vince looked at the boy; his face was white as snow. He staggered, and Vince shot out a steadying arm. "What's the matter, my boy? Come have a seat." He pulled him over to the chair, but Luke tore away from him.

"No, no! Where's Mom? Something terrible has happened!" He yelled these words, which alerted Joan who had been laboring over the books in the other room. She pushed back from her desk, and hurried toward them.

"Luke...what's wrong?"

"Mom...." His face had turned pallid.

"What is it, Luke? You're scaring me!" She grabbed his shoulders and shook him.

"Joan, take it easy." Vince put a restraining arm on her.

"Kyle. It's Kyle." Luke looked at this mother. His mouth was tight and grim. "Kyle's plane has crashed into the ocean."

"What? How? Where? He's supposed to come home *tonight.*" She tried to focus. Take it all in. Nothing made sense. Her heart beat like a drum and ice-cold fear clutched at her stomach. She'd almost lost Kyle the last time he went missing, not so long ago. *Dear God, not again. Please keep my son safe.*

Luke's words reached her from a distance. "He caught a plane at Helgoland, to take him to the mainland, and it crashed right after take-off." The words came fast. "We got a phone call from the authorities over there. They've rescued both the pilot and Kyle and transported them to a hospital in Cuxhaven." He dug into his pocket and pulled out a small piece of paper. "Here, this is the phone number that will get us in touch with the doctor in Germany."

Joan did not hear his last words; she had fainted in Vince's arms.

"Hello, hello," Vince spoke fast. "I'm calling on behalf of Mrs. Joan Weldon. She needs to speak with her son, Kyle Weldon, immediately." There was a pause. "Yes, Kyle Weldon is the name," Vince repeated.

"Just a minute," the hospital receptionist put him on hold. Vince glanced at Joan who sat quietly in the chair, her eyes clinging to his face. He nodded encouragingly. After what seemed a very long time, a man's voice reached Vince's ear.

"Mrs. Weldon, this is Dr. Reiterman..."

"I'm obviously not Mrs. Weldon..."

"I'm sorry. Are you a relative?"

"No."

"I must speak with a relative."

"Just a minute." Vince handed the phone to Joan. "He needs to speak with you."

She took the phone and slowly brought it to her ear.

"This is Joan Weldon. I'm Kyle's mother."

"Right," the doctor said. "Mrs. Weldon, your son was rescued by a fishing boat near the coast of Helgoland along with the pilot of the plane. I have examined Kyle, he has no external injuries but I regret to have to tell you, he suffers from amnesia."

"Amnesia?"

"Yes. It is my opinion he suffers from retrograde amnesia."

"What does this mean? Does he know who he is? Will he recognize me?"

"Retrograde amnesia means the victim can recall events after a trauma responsible for the amnesia, but cannot remember previously familiar information or the events preceding the trauma."

"Oh my God…" The receiver fell into her lap and her hands covered her mouth. Vince quickly picked up the phone.

"Doctor," he said, "Mrs. Weldon is not feeling well, please talk to me."

The doctor re-iterated everything he had told Joan. Luckily, the doctor's English was almost perfect.

"I'm going to keep him another 24 hours and then he'll be released. Is Mrs. Weldon making arrangements to bring him home?"

"Look, Doctor, I'm a close friend of the family. Is it okay if I fly to Cuxhaven and pick up Kyle?"

"Yes, that's agreeable with me. I want Kyle to see a doctor when he gets home. Cognitive rehabilitation will be helpful in learning strategies to cope with memory impairment. There is always the possibility of Kyle getting his memory back. I've seen it happen many times."

"I'll discuss it with Mrs. Weldon and get back to you."

"That's fine. You have my number."

"Thank you for your time. By the way, your English is excellent."

Vince heard a slight chuckle.

"I was fortunate to spend my internship at your famous Mayo Clinic in Rochester, Minnesota. It gets very cold there in the winter."

"You're right about that. "Goodbye, Doctor, I'll be in touch."

"*Auf Wiedersehen*," the doctor said and hung up.

———◆———

The fasten seatbelt sign was on, and Vince buckled up. Out of the corner of his eye he watched Kyle comply as well. Below the Portland International Jetport bustled, its bright lights reaching high up to the sky.

In his mind, Vince relived the last few days since he had spoken with Dr. Reiterman. There had been no doubt in his mind, he would be the person to fly to Cuxhaven and accompany Kyle back to the U.S.A. When he was finally able to convince Joan, and she agreed to his suggestion, he purchased a round trip ticket, including an additional return ticket for Kyle.

As soon as he arrived at Cuxhaven, he checked into a hotel near the airport. Early the next morning, he went straight to the hospital. Deep down he still had hopes, that the doctor was wrong and Kyle might recognize him. When he entered Kyle's room, he was having lunch.

"Hello, Kyle. I'm Vince Rappell."

Kyle looked up and studied Vince's face. He scrunched his forehead and shook his head. "I'm afraid I don't recognize you."

"I know. We have plenty of time to get acquainted. They told me you're being released today. I've booked a flight back to the States that leaves late this afternoon."

Kyle pushed his tray aside. "This food is horrible."

"Let's go have lunch somewhere else. I saw plenty of restaurants on the way over to the hospital. How's that sound?"

"Great. Let's go." Kyle picked up a plastic bag containing soap, toothpaste, and a comb. "They want me to take this home with me." He walked over to the trashcan dropped the bag inside.

"Do you have any other baggage? Where is your camera?"

"Camera?" He raised his eyebrows. "They told me my baggage was lost in the ocean."

"Aha," Vince nodded significantly. They walked out the door and Vince said over his shoulder, "How's the pilot doing?"

"He didn't make it. I don't remember him." Kyle said casually.

They left the hospital, walked half a block and arrived at a small restaurant. They were led to a table by the window and sat down. After the waitress had taken their order, Kyle said, "I understand you know me quite well but I don't have a clue who you are. Not remembering anything feels very strange to me."

"I know," Vince tried to assure him, but Kyle just smiled.

"No, you don't."

"You're right, I don't, but I'm going to fill you in as much as I can. By the time we arrive in Portland, I want you to be able to recognize your mom and brother." He pulled out an envelope containing photos of Joan, Gregg, and Luke.

Kyle studied them intently as Vince began to speak. After a fifteen-minute biography, he paused.

"Well, that's pretty much all I know to tell you." Vince leaned back in his chair and raised the coffee cup. Kyle had remained quiet the entire time.

"Do you have any questions, Kyle?"

"Did I have a girlfriend...or a wife?"

"No wife. A girlfriend? I don't know. This is a question you have to ask your mom." Vince checked his watch. "We must go. Our flight leaves at 5:00 this afternoon." He waved to the waitress, and she arrived with the check. He put the money onto the table and they left. Walking behind Kyle, Vince looked at his straight back and wondered why he didn't ask more questions. There must be so many things he would want to discover. It was almost as if he didn't care to know or was afraid to ask. He made a mental note to talk to Joan. She may have some clue why her son doesn't seem to show much interest in the past.

The plane landed on time. Joan and Luke waited outside the gate. "There he is!" Luke said. "Kyle," he cried and waved with both arms. Vince and Kyle approached, and Joan threw her arms around Kyle and hugged him tightly. "I'm so glad to see you. I've been so worried." He remained stiff as a board inside her arms, and she stepped back.

"I'm sorry, I should have known. You don't remember me."

"I don't, but I'm glad to see you again." Kyle turned to Luke. "Hello, little brother. You and I have lots to talk about."

Joan watched wordlessly and fought hard to keep back her tears. Vince took her by the arm. "Let's go home. It's been a long day."

The next weeks found Joan living in a nightmarish fog. Kyle was polite, but there was no familiarity and he rejected any attempt Joan made to establish the close mother and son relationship they used to share. At least he got on great with Luke and rather than just brothers, they had become good friends.

He saw the doctor three times a week. Although he assured Joan that the possibility of Kyle getting all or at least some of his memory back existed, there was no sign of it yet. One day she surprised him with a camera. She had purchased it several days before and finally got the courage to give it to him. He showed an immediate interest; it was the first time he got excited over anything.

"Gee, thanks, Joan…Mom…" he said and ran out the door and down the beach. He was gone for several hours. When he returned he told her how happy she made him. "I took countless photos and strange as it may sound, the camera felt perfectly comfortable in my hand and I knew how to work it, how to shoot the best angles. I don't remember it clearly, but I know I have taken pictures before, many pictures."

"You have," she said and pulled out the scrapbook she was keeping for him. He looked at it with great interest, and asked many questions.

One morning after he completed his therapy, Kyle left the doctor's office, strolled down Main Street and passed the Mother Goose Nursery. Lisa walked out the door and stopped. He glanced at her and the Mother Goose sign above the door and kept on walking. She turned and leaned against the brick wall. With her face buried in her arm, she sobbed. When someone stopped to check if she was all right, she pulled herself together and said, "I'm fine. Thanks for asking," and hurried on her way.

It had been three months since Kyle's plane crash, but Lisa hadn't spoken to him once. Joan had cautioned her to stay away until he felt more comfortable with his unfamiliar surroundings.

Lisa stopped at the drugstore to pick up her prescription. She passed the magazine section. Her eyes fell on a copy of the National Geographic. She reached for it and leafed through it. Tears flooded her cheeks as she looked at Kyle's photos. The article centered on the plight of the homeless in America's cities and spread across eight pages. Prefaced with Kyle's bio, it ended with: *On March 28, the Cessna 172 carrying Kyle Weldon and Helmut Kullmann, the pilot, disappeared from radar after reporting engine trouble. A fishing boat rescued Kyle and the pilot. The pilot later died, but Kyle returned to his hometown, Graceville, suffering from amnesia.*

She clutched the magazine close to her chest with one hand, and her other hand moved to her belly. She smiled through her tears as she felt the baby move.

———————

Vince and Joan decided to give a party for friends and family to announce their engagement. Vince closed the restaurant early that Saturday and the guests began arriving about five o'clock. They gathered in the huge dining room where the tables and chairs had been moved to the side, to make room for the band. The buffet flanked the dance floor. Vince went all out, having his cook fix ham, roast beef, fried chicken, steamed shrimp and lobster, many side dishes, a salad bar, and a dessert table. The open bar offered an excellent selection of wines, champagne, and beer. As the band played music from the fifties, several couples had moved onto the dance floor.

Lisa stood chatting with Vince when she spotted Kyle watching her from across the room. She blushed and had trouble concentrating on what Vince was saying. She turned to look at Vince who was telling her about the surprise honeymoon he'd planned for Joan. "I'm taking her to Bermuda. She always wanted to go...." He raised his eyes and paused. Lisa spun around and faced Kyle.

"May I have this dance?" Kyle said, and turning to Vince, he added, "You don't mind if I take her away from you, do you?"

"No, not at all."

Lisa stood still; her breath inaudible. Vince gave her a slight push and quickly walked away. There was a bounce in his step.

Kyle took her hand and they walked onto the dance floor. He put his arm around her while the band played "Only You."

"I love this song," she murmured.

"Me too, Lisa."

She looked up and her eyes met his. "Kyle?"

He cupped her face and kissed her. "Remember the Belvedere Hotel?" he whispered. She smiled mutely while he held her close to him.

After the music stopped, Kyle lifted his head and his eyes searched the room. Standing next to Vince, Joan looked at Kyle, and raised her hand to wave, but hesitated. His arm wrapped around Lisa, Kyle nodded, and gave Joan a big smile. All the tension was gone from his face, and then he blew her a kiss.

Karin Harrison was born in Germany but has lived in the United States for over fifty years. Leaving her successful career in the optical field to go back to college, she focused on becoming a writer, and her short stories have since been published in anthologies, literary journals, and online. She has also authored two novels, *Hermann's Ruhe* and *The Wrath of the North Star.*

Harrison lives in Bel Air, Maryland, with her husband.